of love and dragons

DRAGONKYN MATES BOOK ONE

JENN D. YOUNG

Published by Jenn D. Young

Edited by Alicia Torrez

Proofread by Angel Nyx of Horus Proofreading

Design by Get Covers

 Created with Vellum

This book began with a song....
"Dance With The Dragon" By Dark Sarah
Use what inspires you and go for it.
Thank you to my Mom for always supporting me.
Thank you to my amazing author friends and members
of this community for being the loving souls that you are.
Your encouragement means the world.

prologue

ALERIA

COLD SANK deep into my bones as I wrapped my arms around my knees and drew them up to my chest, the hollowness I felt inside gnawing away at my sanity. I had betrayed the person that had looked at me like I mattered most in this world. Why? Because of my family. I had always known that they would cause my downfall, and here I was, trapped in a cold prison cell because of them. I deceived him and now I would be punished. Pain radiated from my chest, the thought of never seeing him again made me nauseous. I would make my family pay for the pain that they had caused me. Tears fell down my cheeks as the despair overwhelmed me.

How was I going to survive this?

one

"ALERIA, come downstairs now, everyone is gathered," my mother shouted, echoing throughout the old house. I made a face of disgust and rose from my desk. A few deep breaths and I was ready to make my way into the figurative Lion's Den.

I forced a smile as I mingled and made small talk with the men and women that knew my parents. The entire party was a demonstration of power and wealth. Our vast home was adorned with large paintings and statuary, the food that was being served was of the finest quality, and the top shelf alcohol flowed freely. It was nothing but a grand facade.

"Aleria…" Disdain dripped from my mother's voice as her eyes trailed over my dress. Her blood-red nails tapped against the glass in her hand, her lip curling before she took a sip of her champagne. "...that is a horrible color on you. Why didn't you wear the dress I had set out?"

"It didn't fit," I muttered. She knew that; purposefully getting a dress that was a size too small in an effort to make me feel insecure in my body.

"Well, dear, if you would stop eating so much, then maybe you would be able to lose that weight and fit into a dress of the proper size." She walked away, laughter echoing behind her.

Swiping my sweaty palms on the fabric of my dress, I snatched a flute of champagne from a waiter as he walked by. My anger dulled as the minutes passed, and I conversed with the familiar strangers. The snide comments of the company in the room did not hit their mark after my mother's caustic remarks. I was used to their insults and passive aggressive complaints about my shortcomings as their eldest daughter.

The faces in the crowd blended together as I drank the bubbly liquid slowly, smiling and nodding when appropriate. I didn't listen to the conversations; the words went in one ear and out the other. They were all about the latest trends in the fashion or financial markets, things that never interested me. Continuing to attend these boorish events was not my choice. I only attended because my absence would have been frowned upon.

My ears perked up as I heard the whispers of a group of girls just a few years younger than my twenty-one-year-old self.

"Did you see how gorgeous Maximos looked?" one of the girls gushed, putting a hand over her heart as she fanned herself with the other.

"Yes!" They all squealed in response. "When he was holding his daughter, it was just to die for."

I blanched in horror. Their chorus of laughter was anything but subtle, and as I realized their topic of discussion, they needed to be more discreet. I gave them a withering look, arching a brow in question while signaling across my throat in a cutting motion.

Abruptly ceasing their mirth, their faces paled as they moved apart and returned to their parents sides.

The girls could only be discussing the photos released of one of the Dragonkyn warriors and his infant daughter. I had seen the photos myself and agreed with the girls, but this was not the place to be discussing such matters.

I was ten years old when the Dragonkyn arrived. They had come from another planet thousands of lightyears away, reaching Earth after their home world was destroyed. Due to environmental instability and a shift in their planets core, their world was no longer able to support life.

Once it became clear to the people of the planet Drakona, their king had sent out ships to try and find the closest planet that would support their lives and way of living. He found Earth just a few short months before the planet collapsed and became a neutron star.

They had wished for peace among our kind, showing us their technology in exchange for asylum for their people. The proud Dragonkyn had shown the people of Earth what their advanced tech could accomplish, quickly propelling our planet into the same realm of space travel.

The partnership had been truly beneficial. The Dragonkyn warriors had found mates among the human women to replenish their depleted population, and Earth had been thriving under their superior medical and technological advances.

"Aleria." My father appeared, taking my arm in a firm hold, and pulling me to the side with him, distracting me from my musings.

"Yes, Father?" It took every ounce of strength I had within me to keep the bite of sarcasm out of my tone. My father was a brutish man, short in stature with dull brown eyes and a receding hairline that he desperately tried to hide.

He sneered at me, drawing up an elegant lip as his brow furrowed in disgust at me. "You look like a trollop. But I guess that is to be expected." Yet another insult, one I had heard countless times before.

My uncle opened the door to the study, glass of alcohol in his hand, and smiled down at me, the look in his eyes anything but familial. "Frederik, this is exactly what we need. She will be perfect."

What the hell was he talking about?

Father chuckled before leveling me with a wilting glance. "I suppose you are right, Gustav." He grasped my upper arm firmly before jerking me into the study.

Wincing in pain, I tried to drag my arm away from his grip. "Father, you are hurting me."

Gustav and Frederik both howled in laughter as they shut the heavy wooden door behind us.

two

ALERIA

FATHER DEPOSITED me into a familiar wingback chair and settled his palms on my shoulders from behind me, securing me in place. Blocking any hope of escape. My uncle took the chair opposite me and leered at me while stroking his thick brown beard. His cheeks were ruddy and pink from the scotch he consumed so heavily. Gustav Mikkelsen was a man who was as wide as he was tall, with a rounded stomach, and more hair on his face than was on his head. I shuddered every time he glanced at me, feeling his gaze crawl over my flesh, making me want to vomit.

"Now Aleria," Uncle began, his eyes lingering on my cleavage. "It is past time for you to be useful to the Brotherhood."

From the moment that the Dragonkyn arrived on Earth, my family had hated the sight of the proud warriors. I could never understand why they had harbored such a hatred for such a peaceful race that was just doing what they could to survive. My father and uncle had banded together with several of their comrades to form the Brotherhood.

The Brotherhood for a Pure Society had the mission of keeping the races separate. They knew that the Dragonkyn were desperate for women to grow their rapidly dwindling population and as such, the Brotherhood did everything in their power to stop the matings from occurring. While they were a hidden, covert organization, the Brotherhood had their hands in a number of different branches of government. They made it their number one objective to get rid of the aliens.

"You live here, enjoying the vast benefits of the wealth of the family, but contribute nothing," he continued.

My anger rose and I bit the inside of my cheek until the metallic taste of blood flooded my mouth. I took care of most of the day-to-day operations required to run the house, as mother couldn't be bothered with communicating with the maids and other household staff. She felt she was above them. I was the one who made sure that the staff was paid, the menus were approved, the schedules were made, and the house was kept in top shape.

"We will finally have our opportunity to make our way into the heart of those bastards' inner-circle. You, my dear, are going to be that opportunity." My uncle smiled widely, his eyes gleaming with malice.

"What the hell are you talking about?" I snapped, unable to keep quiet.

My father dug his nails into the flesh of my shoulders so hard I knew there would be bruises in the morning. "My darling daughter, haven't you heard?" His smile was pure evil. "The twin dragon brothers are finally hosting their own ball with the intention of finding a mate. Those filthy bastards are finally coming of age."

The twins that he referred to were Alexandros and Drakon, the only sons of King Dimitros. They were the youngest of the Dragonkyn and last born before the planet Drakona collapsed. They were just fifteen years old when they arrived on Earth, still reeling from the loss of their mother just a few months earlier. The king had shielded them from the public eye as best that he could, maintaining their privacy to grieve and grow.

Upon their first appearance to the general public at age eighteen, I was immediately obsessed with the teenage princes. They held themselves with a regal, yet friendly air, much like their father. And they were so handsome. Long black hair, strong angled jaws and arched brows with deep midnight blue eyes. They were every woman's fantasy.

I couldn't help my sharp intake of breath at the thought, drawing myself back into my uncle's words.

"And you, my dear, are going to make yourself very available for them," he sneered at me.

"I won't be your whore." I lifted my chin in defiance, meeting his gaze, fire in the depths of my eyes. There was no way that I would do this. I couldn't.

Laughter filled the room. "You seem to think you have a choice, dear Aleria." He drew his stubby fingers down my cheeks, causing a shiver of revulsion to run down my spine and nausea to overwhelm me. Seven hells, how I hated this man. I tried to jerk my face away, but he held firm to my chin.

"Why do you hate them so much?" I implored, my voice barely above a whisper.

My uncle and father laughed, holding their bellies, looking at me as if I sprouted a second head. "You silly, naïve girl. Those filthy dragons are polluting our blood. The species are to remain separate. They are no better than animals," Uncle spat.

I wiped my cheek in disgust as a droplet of spittle hit my skin.

"I have never trusted them or their technology. Just another way to enslave us," my father continued, nodding his head in agreement.

"You are wrong." I said, raising my chin in defiance. "They just want peace. Can't you see that?"

He tisked as he patted my face. "If you want your darling sister to keep receiving the generous medical care that we provide her, you will do as instructed. The ball has been announced for Halloween, just a few weeks away. An invitation has already been secured for you."

"You're a fucking bastard," I bit out through clenched teeth, not able to help the insult that left my lips.

A crack echoed through the room as his palm slapped my cheek. My neck ached with the force of the snap as I brought my hands up to cup my face. A ferocity unlike anything I had ever felt before welled up within me. Angry tears gathering in my eyes that I refused to let fall clouded my vision. My uncle looked triumphant across from me as he took in my appearance, thinking me defeated.

Oh, I would play his games alright. But we would see who would come out on top when the ashes cooled. My fury drove me. I would make them pay for this. The wheels were already turning in my mind as to how I would accomplish my revenge.

"Aleria, you will respect your uncle, as we have raised you to do. Another outburst and the punishment will be exacted against Sariah." My bastard father had the nerve to carry a note of glee in his tone as he spoke. They knew they could never get my obedience with physical attacks against my own person, so the threats were always made against my little sister, Sariah. I couldn't care less about myself. Sariah was my main reason for living in this hellish place.

Sariah was born when I was five years old with a rare genetic condition which caused her immune system to be susceptible to attack, and any little virus or germ that entered her environment could be fatal. Last year she had spent almost six weeks in the hospital with pneumonia as a result of a simple cold. It almost killed me to see her so helpless in that hospital bed day in and day out.

The only reason that my parents kept up with her treatments was to maintain their image with their friends. How bad would it look in their circle if one of their daughters had perished because of their own negligence?

Lowering my head, I feigned defeat, knowing in my heart that this was all temporary. At least that was the dream I always strove toward. My jaw ached with the effort I used to keep it shut, my tongue itching to give them a few choice words.

"Now that we have that settled," Uncle clasped his hands together as he rose from his chair, smiling, "I don't care which of the filthy twins you seduce. Screw both of them for all I care. Once you gain access to their home, you will begin the search for a very important artifact that the Brotherhood has learned of."

Curiosity piqued, I watched him as he approached the wet bar and poured himself another drink. I'm sure he has already had quite enough of the fine scotch, but Gustav never knew when to say no to a good stiff drink. "What kind of artifact?"

"You don't need to know anymore about that just yet. Your goal is to get yourself into their bed and then into their home. We will instruct you from there." He took a long, lingering appraisal of my body from head to toe. "I'm sure you will have no trouble getting them into your bed, girl. You'll just have to learn how to keep that mouth of yours shut long enough to get into their home. Well, unless you are opening it for an entirely different reason." Thinking himself funny, he laughed loudly at the joke and sipped his alcohol.

"She better be really good in bed, otherwise this plan will fail," Father murmured, finally releasing my shoulders. I rolled the joints in them when I was finally free, trying to restore some of the blood flow as my fingers tingled from the punishing grip he had.

"With that body, Frederik, and that attitude of hers, I'm sure the dragon will have his hands full." The creep didn't lift his eyes from my chest as he said the words and licked his lips in anticipation.

I needed to get out of the room, and fast.

"May I be excused now?" I asked, using my best meek and mild tone, dropping my eyes to convey a submissive demeanor.

"Leave us, girl." Father dismissed me with a wave of his hand. "But don't forget what will happen if you run away or fail us on this mission," he added, severity bleeding from his words.

I nodded as I rushed out the door, ignoring the rest of the partygoers as I hurried up the stairs. I vaguely heard my mother call out for me, but I breezed past her, intent on getting to Sariah. She would be the only one that could calm the storm within me, who could help me understand this task which was forced upon me.

Closing the door to her room softly behind me, I gazed at my sixteen-year-old sister as she sat next to her window, reading her tattered copy of The Odyssey, brow furrowed in concentration. Her dark brown hair was arranged in a messy ponytail behind her head, strands of hair scattered all about her face. Her skin looked particularly pale today, the black circles under her hazel eyes more pronounced as she hadn't been getting much sleep.

"What are you up to, Monkey?" My tone lightened, trying to cheer her up as I reached her side, leaning down to plant a soft kiss on her forehead.

"Same thing I always do on party night, Ria, I'm watching people come in and out of the house while I read." She sighed, pressing her face into the cool glass, watching the scene below. Her room overlooked the front courtyard of the house, and she had a perfect view of the long driveway and the cars that arrived during the many social engagements our parents hosted.

"You are lucky you don't have to talk to these people, Ari. They are vile." I lifted the skirts of my simple champagne colored dress and sat down on the window seat, facing her. I lowered my head, placing my chin on top of my knees. "They want me to seduce a dragon. But get this—not just any dragon." I paused, swallowing thickly as the words caught in my throat. "One of the princes. Father and Uncle want me to seduce and honeypot one of the fucking prince dragons so that I can weasel my way into their house to find some fancy artifact thing they want." The angry tears returned to my eyes, but this time I couldn't help them falling down my cheeks. "You know how much I've always idolized them. I can't imagine doing this to them. Why do they hate them so much, Ari? What did they ever do to any of us? All they want to do is live their lives!" I wanted to scream the words, but I knew that my parents had ears everywhere in this house, so I whispered instead. "They are the opposite of humans—they treat their women so well. They are wonderful fathers. You should see the latest episode of Dragon Daddies. Maximos was so adorable playing with his daughter." I wished that I could have a father that treated me half as well as those dragon fathers adored their babies.

Sariah reached out a hand, intertwining her fingers with mine and giving a light squeeze. "Aleria, you need to just leave. Run away," she choked out, her own tears beginning to form in the depths of her hazel eyes. "You can't keep staying for me. I'm not worth it." She shook her head, eyes pleading with me to finally take her advice. She had been begging me for years to just leave her, to quit sacrificing my life for hers.

"Don't say that. I can't leave you little Monkey." I gathered her into my arms and held her tight as we both let the tears flow freely. "You never have to worry about me leaving you. I will always be here, Sariah. Always."

Scooping her small frame into my arms, I carried her to her bed. She had fallen asleep about thirty minutes after our emotional outburst. They rarely happened anymore, but after the revelations of tonight, it was warranted. Sariah tired easily; her body was not able to handle stress such as extreme emotions. I placed her on the soft mattress and swiftly changed my clothes before crawling into bed next to her. We would both need the comfort of each other tonight.

My head hit the pillow and I slipped off into a fitful sleep, my dreams filled with dragons staring down at me with glowing blue eyes, sharp talons closing around me as we flew through the sky. The wind rushed through my ears and stung my face as the strong, beautiful black dragon flew through the air. His rumble of laughter was the only sound that I heard before his talons expanded, releasing me, and I plummeted down toward the earth. I shot straight up in bed just as I landed on the Earth, falling to my death.

three

XANDER

WAKING FROM A NIGHTMARE, my dragon rumbled deeply inside of my chest. He had been in a tizzy lately. The closer it got to my twenty-fifth birthday, the more difficult it was to contain him within. The dream had been strange. He had a girl, no, a woman, clasped in his talons as he flew through the sky. The cool air felt heavenly on his wings, but for some reason, an emotion overtook him that made him release his grip on his precious cargo and watch in horror as she careened down toward Earth.

"What is a dream like that supposed to mean?" I scrubbed my hands over my face, throwing off the sodden sheets as I climbed to my feet. From what I could remember of the woman, she was utterly beautiful. Dark auburn hair fell in waves down her back and around her heart shaped face. Piercing, intelligent green eyes spit fire at me before I had gathered her up in my claws and took flight. She even had an adorable sprinkling of freckles along her nose and cheeks.

Great, now my cock was awake too. "Fuck." I cursed as I walked across the floor to the large shower.

Descending the stairs forty-five minutes later, I still couldn't shake the dream or the woman that I'd seen and let die. Maybe my father would know the significance of the dream? Perhaps it was just a side effect of getting closer to my twenty-fifth birthday.

When a dragon reached the age of twenty-five, he was fully matured and his dragon fully developed. It was at this point where his powers were revealed and the bond between his human soul and his dragon soul merged together. Together, the merged soul could find their mate, the one person who would complete them and provide balance to the darkness within.

"Xander," Drake, my twin brother, shouted from the other end of the large dining room as I entered, "heads up." He tossed me an apple, which I caught in one hand and took a large bite of before smiling.

"Thanks, bro." I gave him a high five as I grabbed a plate and loaded it with the various breakfast items that our chef and head of the house, Hilde, had prepared for us this morning. "Damn, did she make us her orange glazed cinnamon rolls?" I groaned in anticipation as I shoveled two of the delicious treats onto my already full plate.

Another perk of being a dragon was an extremely high metabolism. We had to consume a lot of calories to maintain our bodies, especially when we shifted. Drakon and I were royal Black dragons, meaning that we were the largest and most powerful of all the dragon clans.

The other dragons of our kind were a variety of colors and had various abilities. Blue dragons held power over the elements and could command water and ice. Red dragons were masters of fire and the purple dragons held very strong psychic abilities. Only black dragons possessed power over all the elements, hence our rule over the Dragonkyn. Our father, Dimitrios, was the king, maintaining the balance and ensuring that our laws were obeyed.

He was a kind, generous and fair king, always listening to his people and providing judgments that all could abide by. Since the environmental collapse of our planet, caused by the shifting of the planet's core—and our subsequent departure for earth—he had been the pillar of strength for the Dragonkyn. Shortly before our actual departure, a series of natural disasters rocked the planet, causing total chaos and massive casualties.

Our mother had been one of those casualties.

Since her death, our father hadn't been the same person. He still ruled, still maintained the order and peace, but nothing brought him joy. His mate was gone, and he was a dragon without the light to balance his soul. My own heart ached when I thought of my beautiful mother.

"Earth to Xander." Drake tossed a piece of scrambled egg into my face, which landed square on the bridge of my nose. It caused him to snicker before he dug back into the food on his plate. "Stop brooding," he said, mouth full of bacon, the remaining half piece he used to point at me. "You have that look on your face that says 'I'm thinking too much' like always."

Hilde walked through the swinging door to the kitchen and gaped in horror at Drake. "Drakon Rathnar Scwartzen how many times have I told you not to speak with your mouth full?" She approached him, her deadly wooden spoon in hand.

Drake's eyes widened as he looked at the barely

five-foot-tall spitfire of a woman that had been running our house since shortly after our arrival on Earth. "Hilde, I'm sorry. You know I didn't mean to." He turned his charming grin on the woman, knowing full well that it never worked on her. I couldn't help the small laugh that escaped my mouth.

Thwack!

She brought down the spoon on the back of his hand. "Ow!" he shouted.

"Manners, Drakon. Manners. Your father raised you boys as gentlemen and I expect you to act as such," she scolded. The familiar words were forced into our heads, not that we needed them. Honor was a staunch value among dragons, and manners and respect were deeply ingrained in our upbringing as Dragonkyn. We just liked to have a bit of fun and rattle Hilde from time to time.

Thwack!

This time it was his bicep. "You are princes of the house of Black Dragons." Thwack! "You will" Thwack! "Chew with" Thwack! "Your mouth shut" Thwack!

The final blow landed, and I howled with laughter. Poor Drake looked contrite after Hilde laid into him.

27

My laughter quickly died as she turned toward me with fire in her eyes, "And you, no laughing or antagonizing your brother. I know you, Alexandros, you egged him on." My gaze didn't leave the deadly spoon she waved about in her hands, accenting each of her words in a threatening manner as she approached me.

"Yeah, Xander, don't antagonize me," Drake taunted, sticking his tongue out, acting like a child rather than the almost twenty-five-year-old dragons we were.

Hilde just sighed, shaking her head, muttered something neither of us could make out as she left the room through the swinging door.

"So, brother, what has you in such a tizzy this morning? Another dream?" Drake arched an eyebrow at me, setting his fork down and leaning back in his chair.

I raked my fingers through my hair in agitation as I told him of the dream. "I have never seen her face before last night. I mean, I know it was the same woman, but before it was just flashes, her scent, the flow of her hair, a glimpse of her eyes. I don't understand why I drop her. I feel such a connection to her, why would I kill her? It doesn't make any sense."

Drake narrowed his eyes, considering my words carefully. "And your other dreams of this woman?"

I groaned. "Nothing as intense or detailed as last night. This time, I saw her fully, and fuck Drake, she was beautiful. Her eyes, her hair, her body." I sank down into the seat and looked upward, squeezing my eyes shut tightly, imagining her curves.

"Dude, it sounds like she is your mate," Drake whispered hesitantly.

The words caused me to still. I hadn't even thought of that possibility. We had heard of times where dragons had premonitions or dreams of their fated before meeting, but never before reaching the age of maturity. It was why the thought had never even crossed my mind. This was beginning to be much more complicated than I first expected. I needed to have a discussion with my father. He would know something. He had to.

"Damn it, Drake, if that is the case, then this fucking sucks," I answered, letting my fork fall against my plate with a clatter. Because the foreboding feeling I got when dropping her to her death made it obvious that my dreams were trying to tell me something.

"Yeah, Xander, it does."

* * *

"Enter," my dad's strong voice called from the other side of the door after my knuckles rasped against the dark wood.

"*Pateros*," I hesitated, using the word for Father in our native tongue as Drake and I had always done. "I was wondering if you had a moment?"

I knew he was extremely busy with preparations for the ball as well as trying to pinpoint the movements of the Brotherhood for a Pure Society. The Brotherhood was an anti-Dragonkyn movement that had existed for several years but had made a strong push in the last six months, gaining momentum and followers.

I never understood what the Brotherhood had against us. We did nothing to hurt human society. In fact, we'd done the exact opposite. We shared our technology and scientific knowledge with the humans, allowing them to invent cures to some of their deadliest diseases. They had perfected space travel because of us, cured cancer because of us, yet they were not grateful. Factions like the Brotherhood still insisted we had nefarious intentions behind our arrival on Earth.

"Yes, son, what is it?" He removed the glasses

from the bridge of his nose and held his hand out, gesturing for me to take a seat opposite him.

Sighing, I took my seat and took in his appearance. Lately, I had begun to think the stress of this life was starting to get to him. The lines around his eyes deepened, the dark circles beneath more pronounced. I knew he wasn't sleeping. My father was the strongest person I knew, always carrying the weight of his people on his shoulders, and after losing my mother, he had no one left to share the burden with.

I often wished there was more that I could do to help bear the load.

"I hate to bring this to you, but I need some advice." I hesitated.

"Son," he sighed, rubbing his temples. "I have always told you and your brother that no matter the significance, you can come to me with anything. Now what is it that has you in such knots?" His lips curled up slightly in a semblance of a smile, seeing right through me.

"I've been having a recurring dream. Not the same dream mind you, but of the same person." I paused. "A woman."

He leaned forward in his chair, his amber eyes

glowing with excitement. "Tell me about her, Alexandros."

"At first, I never saw her face or even her body, it was as if she was stuck in a fog, but I felt her. Her presence would overwhelm me." He nodded his approval. "Then last night, I saw her. She was the most beautiful woman I have ever laid eyes on and something inside me snapped." I swallowed harshly, trying to find a way to go on to the next part of the dream.

"But then, something happened. I shifted into my dragon. I scooped her up in my talons and we were flying through the sky. Then, I released her. I let her go. Let her fall down to the ground and her death." I couldn't meet his gaze. I dropped my head down in shame and clenched my fists. "How could I have done something like that, *Pateros*? Why?"

He leaned back in his chair, exhaling deeply, his eyes calm. "Alexandros, it was just a dream, it doesn't mean anything." I couldn't believe the words. His tone when he said them didn't sit quite right with me. He knew more than he let on.

"You have always said that dreams can be a premonition." I narrowed my eyes at him, trying to determine what he was hiding.

"They can, but not always. It doesn't sound like

it in this case, my son. I wouldn't worry about it." He waved his hand in a dismissive gesture. "You have two weeks until your birthday, you have enough on your plate to worry about. This dream is nothing more than a stress induced event. You are simply worried about coming of age and finding a mate. It is perfectly reasonable." He nodded, considering the discussion closed.

Rising from my seat, I blinked in confusion. This is not how I expected this conversation to go. There was something going on with my father, he knew more than he was letting on. "Thank you, *Pateros*. You're probably right. I will go, let off some steam by taking a good long flight." I smiled, although it didn't quite reach my eyes, and turned to leave.

"Alexandros, please do not worry about this, all will be fine." He tried to reassure me.

I nodded without turning back in his direction and shut the door behind me.

four

XANDER

TWO WEEKS LATER

"I HATE WEARING THIS SHIT," Drake remarked, tugging at his cravat in the mirror. "Why *Pateros* insists we always look like we came out of Earth era Regency England I have no idea." He rolled his eyes as he tugged down the ends of his black suit jacket, tails flapping out behind him.

We were both on edge, the ball started the night before our birthday and would stretch past midnight, when we would turn twenty-five and reach our maturity. I knew Drake was just as anxious as I was. There was something about this night, something about this party that was going to happen.

"I feel like this damned thing is choking me." I situated the fancy knot, meeting my brother's gaze in the mirror, grimacing.

"You and me both, brother," he groaned.

"Let's get this over with," I muttered, turning on my heel and leaving the room.

Drake and I plastered on smiles as we stood beside our father, greeting the guests as they arrived. Human and Dragonkyn alike flooded the vast ballroom for what was deemed the party of the decade. Many of our kind had been waiting years for us to reach our maturity, as we were the last remaining children born of our home world.

"My King, thank you so much for the invitation." Maximos shook my father's hand firmly, his infant daughter balanced on his other hip. "This little gorgeous princess is Larissa." He cooed at his daughter, who smiled and giggled in response.

Dimitros smiled widely and took Larissa from her father's arms, holding her up before cuddling her to his chest. The girl planted a wet kiss against his cheek and squealed as his beard tickled her face.

Father had always adored children. He took every opportunity there was to visit with the men who had sired children, spending time with them and getting to know their mates and offspring. Just another reason why he was our beloved ruler.

Maximos laughed as Larissa tugged at the strands of Father's beard. "She is a grabby one, my King, you better watch it." His mate, Anja, joined them, a look of horror on her face as her daughter began tugging in earnest at the king's face.

"Larissa, no." Anja breathed, trying to extract her daughter from his grasp. "I'm so sorry, your majesty, we have been working on having her not grab at things, but..."

We all started laughing. Maximos gathered his mate into his arms and placed a gentle kiss into her hair. "Darling, it is quite alright. Trust me, the king has dealt with much worse than an eight-month-old tugging at his beard." He bent down and whispered more words into her ear.

Anja dropped her eyes, a blush staining her cheeks, and Dimitros continued to bounce the small girl. "Anja, your daughter is utterly beautiful and a wonderful baby. You should be proud."

Our king always did have a way with words. I could see the sheen of tears in Anja's eyes as Maximos tightened his arm around her shoulders. "Thank you, your majesty. She is our pride and joy," she whispered in response.

"Anja, please, call me Dimitros, you don't need to be so formal." He smiled and returned Larissa to her mother. Anja gaped at him, and then turned to her mate, confusion clouding her features. Larissa let out a loud yawn and then squirmed in her mother's arms until she settled against her shoulder.

"Thank you, Dimitros."

My father smiled brightly, giving Anja a small hug before placing a gentle kiss on Larissa's forehead. He shook Maximos' hand again before they departed.

Drake snorted in laughter as he left. "Maximos has grown soft since he mated."

"Shut up," I slapped him across the back of the head. "He is happy. We can only be so lucky." I added, jealousy clear in my voice.

"Thank you, Alexandros," Father smiled, winking at me. "You will both understand more when you find your mates."

"Why do you always pick on me?" Drake sighed as he rubbed the back of his head.

"Oh, boo hoo," I scoffed, teasing him.

"We all know it's the TV show that made him soft," Klaas, the captain of the Elite Dragon Flight, commented as he approached from the right. He wore a soft smile on his face, his dark eyes focused, ever searching the room for threats. Long brown hair was secured with a queue at the back of his neck and he was dressed in his formal armor for the occasion.

"That's right, I forgot about that silly reality TV show that he is on. What is it called again? Baby Daddy?" Drake commented, causing me to laugh.

Drake's deep belly roll laughter answered mine and I even heard Klaas let out a chuckle. "Dragon Daddies, that's what it's called." I finally remembered the title of the show. "God, I can't believe that I agreed to do it with that horrendous title. Whose idea was that anyways?"

"Mine," Father answered, leveling me with a gaze that challenged me to make a further comment.

"Okay, changing subject," Drake said, whistling loudly.

Klaas approached father and whispered something in his ear, to which Father nodded and Klaas returned to his post by the door. "What was that all about?" I asked, cocking my head at my father.

"Nothing you need to be concerned about, Son." He smiled. "Have fun, mingle, meet some women." He clasped a hand on each of our shoulders and squeezed tightly. He turned on his heel and left the room.

"Am I the only one who thought that whole exchange with Klaas very strange?" Drake remarked, taking a long pull from his glass of champagne.

"No, brother. It was strange indeed."

ALERIA

"Fuck," I cursed as I stepped on the hem of my dress. I heard the hiss of the fabric tearing and prayed that it wouldn't be something too noticeable. Damn mother for her dress selection. The black dress flowed in waves off my curvy figure, accentuating my breasts and lush hips, but the hem line was way too long and I was constantly stepping on it. The heels that she had paired with it were too wobbly and I couldn't balance very well.

"Damn it, Mother, I hate you." I gathered the skirts in my fist and made my way up the stairs of the grand house. This place was amazing, a dream come true. I just wish that I could be here under better circumstances.

"Name?" the doorman asked as I approached. My face was flushed with frustration and exertion after climbing the stairs and sweat beaded along my brow.

"Aleria Mikkelsen."

"Thank you, Ms. Mikkelsen, if you would please step this way, we just need to check your clutch to make sure you don't have any weapons." He swept a hand to indicate a table where a security guard, dressed in a fancy black suit, stood.

I smiled and tilted my head in response. I didn't have any weapons, just my phone, make up and a few other items that would be considered harmless. Nothing to hide in there. I opened the small beaded bag and after a quick glance the monster of a man waved me through.

"Wow," I gasped as I glanced up in the ballroom. This place was utterly magical. Crystal chandeliers lined the room, bathing the space in a soft glow. In the middle of the arched ceiling hung a massive piece that had to be taller than my five-and-a-half-foot height. It glittered, throwing rainbows of colors along the painted murals. The portraits showed dragons flying, playing, eating and gathering in peace. I was struck by the details of the wings, the colors of the different dragons as they flew across the room.

"I know that look, this must be your first time here."

I spun around when I heard the deep voice, my pointed heel catching on my skirt again. Large, muscled arms wrapped around my waist, securing me tightly as I laid my hands against the wall of a firm chest.

"Thank—" The rest of the words died in my throat as I looked up at him. It was Alexandros, one of the dragon princes. My heart rate quickened as I explored his features, midnight blue eyes looked at me with concern. His face was regal, with full arched eyebrows, high cheekbones and full lush lips.

"I know you," he breathed, recognition sparking in his expression.

I blinked in confusion. "I'm sorry, your majesty, but I don't believe we have actually met," I whispered.

I felt his chest rumble beneath my fingertips as he growled low and deep in his throat, a shiver running down my spine at the sound. My eyes looked him up and down, taking in his handsome appearance. He looked even more gorgeous in person. His black hair was slicked back from his face, secured at the back of his neck with a simple tie. Crisp white shirt, sable black suit jacket and a maroon old-style cravat centered below his powerful throat. Everything about this man called to the woman inside of me.

"My apologies." He cleared his throat, taking a quick step backward. "My name is Alexandros." He lowered himself into a bow, never taking his intense eyes off my face. Heat crept up my chest and a flush spread over my cheeks.

"Aleria Mikkelsen, your majesty." I held out a hand before realizing that was a socially inappropriate move. I blanched and moved to take my hand back, but Alexandros captured it between his large fingers and brought it to his mouth.

"A pleasure to meet you Aleria. Please drop this 'your majesty' nonsense. We don't have many formalities here." His lips brushed over the bare skin of my knuckles, causing a shiver of excitement to run through me. This man was good. Heat pooled in my lower belly and I clenched my thighs together as he smiled at me, showing just a hint of his perfect white teeth.

"You can call me Alexandros, but I prefer Xander." His pink tongue traced a small line along my skin before releasing me, making me shiver again.

"I-I—" Stammering, my brain would not form a

sentence as I tilted my head back to look at the dragon prince towering over me. "Thank you, Xander," I finally was able to spit out.

"You are very welcome, Aleria." He drew the back of his hand down my cheek, and I savored the feel of his hands upon my body. "I must attend to my father now, but will you save a dance for me, little one?"

I nodded and he smiled in response. "Good. Until later, Aleria." I was rooted in place, watching his lithe form move across the room, the muscles in his legs showcased by his tight breeches, his firm ass drawing my ultimate attention. A shiver of desire ran through me as my heart fluttered in my chest. My response to this man was visceral and primal.

Good lord, I was in trouble.

five
XANDER

I BARELY MADE it out into the garden before my claws exploded. My dragon was roaring from within to be set free so that we could claim the woman, who we had left inside, as our own. In the state I was in, it was impossible for me to hold control over my human form. In the distance, I could hear the clock chime, signaling the arrival of midnight and with it, my maturity. I ran further into the garden, toward the woods, shedding my clothes as my feet pounded against the cold ground.

I collapsed to the soft grass of the clearing, hidden by a thick cover of evergreen trees, just as my dragon took control. I hissed as bones shattered, tendons tore, and my body restructured itself into my dragon form. Snorting, I watched as the smoke left my nostrils, holding back the fire rising in my throat. I couldn't set anything on fire. Father would get very upset if the party abruptly ended because I engulfed the house in flames. I had once ended a garden party by setting the bushes on fire. Drake and Father still didn't let me live that one down.

Fuck. That woman was breathtaking.

The instant I saw her, my blood set to fire inside my veins, my dragon roared in triumph and my cock lengthened behind the zipper of my trousers. There was no doubt in my mind anymore. The woman from my dreams was my mate. And now she was inside my home, waiting for me. She had watched me with the same rapt attention and attraction that I had for her.

A low keening sound left my dragon throat as I thought of her death at my own hands. It didn't have to mean anything. I wouldn't let it mean anything. It wasn't going to happen.

"Xander, where are you? Father is getting anxious. I'm trying to stall him, but you need to return inside."

Drake's voice fluttered through my mind on the familiar psychic link. He knew that I had shifted, sensing my emotions and reaching out along our familiar twin bond. Dragonkyn twins were rare and had deep psychic bonds as a result from sharing a womb. There was only one other set of twins in history, cousins from our mother's side.

"*Tell him I'll be there momentarily. The hour hit me a bit hard.*"

"*That is an understatement brother.*"

He chuckled, causing me to wince.

Forcing my mind to clear, I focused on my dragon and merged with him. We became one as he drew back, and I regained control of my form. I shifted back into my human body, my elbow and knees supporting my weight. The cold seeped into my bones as my muscles protested the quick change. My teeth chattered as I slowly climbed to my feet, my breath coming out in white clouds in front of my face.

"*I left your clothes at the edge of the clearing.*"

I was seriously going to owe Drake at the end of the night. I jogged to where he indicated and dressed swiftly. I knew there would be hell to pay with my father at the end of the night.

Struggling with the damn cravat, I ended up tearing the fabric before tossing it to the forest floor, deciding to forgo it and go with the simple unbuttoned shirt look. I would catch a few dirty looks, but it would be better than being choked by the stupid necktie anyway. Drake had forgotten my socks, causing me to curse again as I put my shoes on.

"Damn it, Drake." I hated shoes to begin with. These boots were uncomfortable as hell without socks on. Grimacing as I walked through the garden, I tucked my shirt into my pants and threw the jacket on.

Spotting her, I stopped dead in my tracks, almost tripping over my own feet. She was standing on the patio, her face frozen in sheer terror for a moment before she took a deep breath and composed herself. Her hand trembled as she took a drink from her champagne glass. My eyes were drawn to her throat, where the muscles contracted as she drank the liquid.

Emerald green eyes found mine in the darkness, trapping me, holding me captive as we couldn't look away from each other. Her auburn hair was gathered elegantly around her head, with tendrils draping down to grace the ivory skin of her neck. I was utterly entranced by this woman. She took a deep shuddering breath, dropping her gaze from mine, breaking the spell between us, before turning and scurrying inside.

Confusion and frustration rolled through me as she broke the connection. A deep rumbling settled in my chest, anger clouding my vision. How dare she turn away from us? She was our mate, destined for me and my dragon, didn't she know that?

Of course, she didn't, you idiot. You barely spoke twenty words to her. Slowly counting to ten to control my temper, I approached the door and returned to my father and Drake.

"What the fuck, dude?" Drake whispered, looking me up and down while handing me a crystal glass full of scotch.

"Don't ask right now," I growled as I threw back the amber liquid, savoring the burn as it settled in my belly. It took a large amount of alcohol to get a dragon drunk due to our advanced metabolism, but I was sure as hell going to try tonight.

"Where have you been, Alexandros? We were supposed to start speeches thirty minutes ago." My father remarked through gritted teeth. His cheeks had slashes of red, relaying his fury to me. He hated to be late.

"I apologize, *Pateros*." I worked every ounce of meekness into my tone. Drake coughed to disguise his laughter, his eyes gleaming with mirth.

My father snorted in response. "I don't care what your silly excuse is, although I am curious how you have lost your tie." He paused and stroked his beard as his eyes narrowed at me. "Let's go, we need to address our guests and then we can begin the dancing."

Drake and I nodded in response and fell in line behind him as he approached the crowd to speak.

He clapped, drawing the attention of the crowd as he stood on the landing overlooking the ballroom. "My honored guests," his loud booming baritone echoed throughout the ballroom. "On behalf of myself and my house, thank you for attending tonight to help us celebrate the twenty-fifth birthday of my beloved sons, Alexandros and Drakon."

The answering applause from the crowd was deafening from our position on the balcony. Drake and I bowed to the crowd to signal our gratitude before Father continued.

"Ever since our arrival on Earth a decade ago, it has been my primary goal to see the peaceful cohabitation of the Dragonkyn and humankind. Our numbers were once bleak, but thanks to the wonderful mates our males have found, we have breathed new life into our people." More applause rang out before my father lifted a hand to silence the crowd, his smile warm.

"Now, my sons have reached their age of maturity, and thus are able to find their mates. It is my sincere hope that they each find their mate and have a long, loving relationship filled with many children." He raised his glass toward Drake and I. "To my boys: may your dragons be strong, your mates be fierce, and your children be healthy."

The dragons in the crowd roared in response, my Father, Drake and I joining in with the familiar family call. The music started up shortly after, and our dragon warriors filed up the stairs to give my twin and I handshakes and hugs of congratulations. While the Dragonkyn spoke of their own maturity parties, my eyes never left the party below, scanning the people, looking for my feisty Aleria, needing her contact.

The world snapped into focus as I found her curvy form close to the exit, my breath leaving my lungs as I excused myself from the other Dragonkyn to get to my mate.

six

I COULD FEEL his eyes on me as I moved about the ballroom, causing me to break out in a flush. When he saw me outside, I nearly fainted, his gaze had been so intense. He looked at me as if he wanted to eat me alive. My libido went into overdrive. In my mind I pictured his dark head between my legs, feasting on my sensitive flesh while his large hands pinned my hips to the bed.

My heart raced in my chest as heat crept up my chest to my cheeks. My breath left my lungs in shaky pants as I wobbled on my feet as I made my way to the restroom. What was it about this man that affected me so much? I had never been a woman ruled by my desires. In fact, I never dated, had barely even kissed a boy much less slept with one.

My father and uncle had no clue that they had sent a virgin to seduce the dragon prince. I groaned in frustration. How much worse could this get?

The bathroom door swung open as I pushed it and I walked through having composed myself. I walked the hallway, eyes on the ground, my hands clutched on my long skirts to prevent me tripping over them once again. Looking down and muttering to myself, I collided into a strong chest. Thick arms wrapped around me, as I gasped and looked up into the eyes of the object of my erotic thoughts.

"Hello, little one. Where have you been hiding?" His voice was smooth as silk, the deep tones sending chills across my body, goosebumps rising along my arms.

"I, um," I licked my lips and swallowed, "had to go to the bathroom." I inhaled sharply and raised my chin, our gazes connecting. The electricity crackled between us as his eyes zeroed in on my lips. My tongue reached out to moisten them again in a reflexive gesture, the answering growl that left his throat causing me to moan.

"Aleria." He whispered, he settled his hands on my hips and dragged me closer into his hard frame, his body bathing me in heat.

"Xander," his name left my lips on a breathy

exhale as his nose drifted along my neck, inhaling my scent.

"I love it when you call me that," he growled, his voice the sexiest thing that I had ever heard in my life.

Giggles drifted up to my ears, breaking the spell that Xander held over me. A group of girls was leaving the bathroom, their eyes wide as they walked by us. I cleared my throat, pushing at the wall of his chest as I took a step back. Their whispers echoed through the hall as they discussed what they saw between the prince and I. It was a sobering moment.

"I'm sorry, I don't know what came over me just now. I apologize for running into you." Formality dripped from my tone as I put on the familiar mask I used with my parents. "If you will excuse me, I must be going."

His hand shot out, circling around my wrist. "Please, Aleria. You still owe me a dance." His lips tilted at the corners and he gifted me with an enchanting smile. Xander could get any woman that he wanted, so why did he want to dance with me?

Are you forgetting that this is your mission? Don't forget Sariah. You must do this.

Yet, the idea of deceiving Xander made my soul

scream in protest. I couldn't explain it. I had just met the man, yet I already felt so connected to him.

Anything for Sariah. That was the goal.

I decided then that I would keep with my meek and shy act, throwing in touches of my inner fire when called for. The dragon would eat it up and hopefully this mission would be over quickly, and I could get back to Sariah and forget any of this ever happened. Although my heart contracted at the thought.

"I suppose I have time for just one dance," I said sweetly, smiling up at him. He returned my smile with one of his own as his hand slid up my arm to cup my cheek.

"One thing first," He said softly, bending his head down toward me. His soft lips descended upon mine with a gentleness that I didn't know existed. I gasped in surprise and he deepened his kiss by running his tongue along mine. I reached my hands up and wound my fingers around his shoulders as I arched my back into his chest. A moan lingered in my throat as our mouths, tongues and teeth dueled with each other. A tangy flavor lingered on my tongue, something that was uniquely Xander; it made me crave more.

He drew back slowly, his lips hovering above me

before he rested his forehead against mine. "Aleria." He whispered against my swollen lips, and I had to fight the sound of pleasure that threatened to echo in the room at the sound of my name leaving his mouth on a hoarse growl.

This man was going to be the end of me, I just knew it.

XANDER

I shouldn't have kissed her. I really shouldn't have. Seeing her perfect pink tongue lick at those plump lips had been my downfall. When she tried to leave, I had to get her to stay, reminding her of her promise to dance with me, but instead I stole a kiss.

Damn, what a kiss it was, too.

She had been hesitant, unpracticed, but followed my lead and fell into a perfect rhythm with me. We were made for each other and I just knew that everything between us would be explosive.

Straightening to my full height, I winced as my erection pressed against the zipper of my slacks. Good thing when I buttoned my coat, it would cover my groin, otherwise that would be fun to explain to the guests.

"Come, darling." I held out a hand and smiled at

her. She returned the smile. I could see the wheels in her mind working as she reached to take my outstretched palm. This woman was up to something, but I couldn't quite place it yet.

She was obviously not comfortable or very familiar with men, and it set my blood on fire to know that I may be one of the only men to have kissed her. I would discover all of her secrets, and I would give her all of mine in return. Together, we would explore each other, body and soul. My cock jumped again at the thought of thoroughly exploring her lush body.

"So, Xander, I have something to confess." She tucked an escaped tendril of hair behind her ear and looked up at me.

"Oh?"

"I don't know how to dance." Color stained her cheeks as she turned away from me in shyness.

I laughed, the rich sound echoing in the hall around us. "That is quite alright, little one. I have a plan." I winked at her, teasing gently.

My hands settled along her waist and lifted her until the front of her heels rested on the tops of my boots. She gasped as she realized my intentions, a tentative smile easing across her face before she placed one hand on the top of my shoulder and laced her fingers through my other.

"Just follow my lead. I won't let anything happen to you." I leaned down and whispered the words against her ear and grinned as I felt the shudder that ran through her body. This woman was perfect.

The music started. The string quartet my father hired had been the best that money could buy. The soft melodic notes flowed over us as I moved to the beat, Aleria secure in my arms, not a care in the world. I held her tightly, the dance making our bodies move and twirl along the marble dance floor. Her breathing accelerated, and a lovely pink color rose along her ample chest and settled in her cheeks. She was lovely when she was flushed. I couldn't wait to see her entire body heated with passion.

"Enjoying the dance so far, Aleria?" I spun her out of my body before using her momentum to twirl her back into the shelter of my arms. Her answering laughter was a soothing balm on my soul, calming me.

"You are an amazing dancer, Xander."

Her voice was intoxicating, flooding over my senses along with her scent as I inhaled from her neck. "You are amazing, *cara*." My lips feathered along her pulse, feeling her soft, hot skin beneath me.

The song ended on a crescendo as I held her body closer to mine.

"Alexandros, why don't you introduce me to this lovely woman you found this evening?" My spine straightened as my father's voice broke through the fog that had settled over me. I heard Aleria's gasp as she looked around me to see who had spoken the words.

"That's the king," she whispered, astonishment making her cling tighter to me. Her delicate nails curled into the fabric of my suit jacket.

"I know, darling. He's my father, or did you forget that?" My hand slid along her waist to settle at the base of her spine, just above the luscious curve of her ass.

She nibbled on her lip as she looked up at me, that adorable blush still staining her cheeks. "Father, this is Aleria Mikkelsen, I just met her this evening. Aleria, this is my father, King Dimitros Schwartzen."

"Your majesty, it is an honor to meet you." Aleria bowed before my father, bending her back low, not making eye contact with him and not straightening her spine until she was sure it was proper.

His booming laughter made her gasp. "My dear girl, we don't do such formalities here." He smiled warmly at her, pulling her into a fierce embrace, his large arms wrapping around her frame, much to her shock. I cleared my throat to stifle my laughter knowing it wouldn't earn me a slap upside the head from my father. Awkwardly, she brought her arms around him and returned the hug, her movements stiff.

"Please call me Dimitros, Aleria. I am sure we will be seeing a lot of each other very soon." Pulling back, he raised her hand to his mouth and kissed her knuckles, his dark amber eyes twinkling with warmth. "I recognize that look in my son's eyes. We are very blessed indeed that you came to our event tonight, Aleria. To meet one's mate on the night of maturity is almost unheard of, but it is a sign from the Gods that this is a blessed pairing." With a warm smile, he placed a soft kiss on her cheek before he placed her hand in mine.

Clasping a hand on my shoulder, he said, "My son, I couldn't be prouder. She is beautiful and I see she has a fierce soul within her. Aleria will make a fine mate for you." He squeezed my hand and I could see the sheen of tears in his dark eyes.

"Thank you, *Pateros*," I whispered softly, pulling

him into a firm embrace. He slapped me on the back before turning and leaving the room.

The grin dropped from my face when I turned to Aleria. She looked utterly terrified as she turned to me, trembling as she whispered, "mate?"

seven

THE KING LOOKED like he was about to explode with happiness as he looked at me, then he began to speak. One word stood out above all the others. Mate. He had referred to me as Xander's mate.

No.

This could not be happening.

Xander couldn't possibly be my mate. Guilt ate at me, turning my stomach as Xander smiled brightly, embracing his father with such ferocity. I placed a firm palm over my belly, trying to stop the nausea that was rolling within me. Attraction clouded my judgment, a result of the bond. I had watched enough of the Dragonkyn reality TV shows to know the effects of the mate bond on the human partner.

This intensity was beyond anything that they had described before. My body felt hot as I looked over the black dragon prince, with his dark hair and sapphire eyes. Everything inside of me screamed to touch him, that I needed him by my side.

What was wrong with me?

Dimitros departed, and Xander turned to me with that sexy as sin grin on his face; the hollowness I felt inside intensified. How could this man that I just met set me on fire with just a glance?

"Mate?" The grin dropped immediately, replaced with a fierce scowl as his brow furrowed.

"Don't tell me you don't feel the connection between us too?" He reached out a hand for me, trying to draw me closer, before I took a hasty step back. Of course, my heel caught on my dress, sending me flying backward. I braced myself for the nasty fall, but Xander saved me by curling an arm around my back.

"Why are you pulling away now?" He cocked his head at me, confusion marring his perfect features, hurt flashing in the depths of his midnight eyes.

"I barely know you," I breathed, sliding my hands up his chest, reveling in the feeling of his muscles bunching and jumping beneath my touch. "I met you an hour ago."

"Then stay and get to know me." His face hovered above mine, lips held a scant inch away. Flames of desire flickered in his eyes, his warm breath washing over my parted lips.

"Not here, Xander," I breathed, eyes darting around, seeing the scene that we had been making on the edge of the dancefloor. A crowd was gathered, their greedy eyes taking us in as we spoke. I was sure they had heard the comments the king had made, maybe even some of them heard him refer to me as Xander's mate.

As if this night could get any worse.

His features hardened as he led me out of the room with a firm hand on the small of my back. The heat from his touch radiated through me, igniting the fire within me. I didn't know if I could resist this man. His passion, his intensity, everything about him reached into my very soul and drew me to him.

Damn it. I squeezed my eyes together tightly, feeling a tear leak down my cheek. I swiped it away quickly, hoping Xander wouldn't see the movement. Why were my emotions all over the place? It was almost as if everything was more intensified, my body on fire, my feelings out of control. The hand that Xander had on the small of my back spread heat throughout my body, making me shake with anticipation.

"Xander, you going to introduce me to your lovely mate?" another distinct voice drawled as we entered a private corridor, causing me to squeak in surprise as it pulled me from my musings.

"Fuck, Drake," Xander growled, the sound sexy. I loved the sound of the curse falling from his lips, it stoked the fierce desire inside me and I almost moaned his name thinking of all the dirty things he could whisper in my ear beginning with that word.

"Shit. You already kissed her?" Drake muttered doubling over in pain, putting a hand on the wall to steady himself. "I'm Drakon, or Drake to those closest to the family. Nice to meet you. I'm going to leave before Xander beats me to death." His twin disappeared into the darkness, causing Xander to breathe out a sigh of relief.

"Little one, I need to get you away from the crowd and the other dragons now. I am not going to be able to control my instincts much longer." His voice was deep, layered with power as he laid his hands on my cheeks and tilted my head up to meet his gaze. "It is already starting. Damn it, I thought we would have more time."

I gasped, his eyes were glowing, shining brightly in the dimly lit hallway. His features appeared sharper, more refined. His pupils were dilated as his gaze traveled from the top of my head to the tips of my toes. Heat pooled between my thighs as his eyes lingered on my breasts.

"Xander," I breathed, feeling as the heat grew too much for me to bear. My fingers itched to reach out and touch him; instead I clenched them into fists at my sides.

"I know, little one. I need to get you up to my room. Now." He lifted me into his arms, sprinting down the hall and up a flight of stairs.

My teeth started to chatter as I couldn't stop my hands from running along the hard muscles of his chest, shoulders and neck as he ran. "What is happening to me, Xander?" I was hot and cold, fire and ice battling their way through my system as all I could think of was Xander buried deep inside my body.

"Damn it, Aleria, your scent is driving me insane," he groaned, a deep pain-filled sound, as he slowed his pace. "Think about the most non-sexy thing you can to calm your scent. We need to have a little chat once we get to my suite."

I squirmed in his arms, my body desperate for

release, for my mate deep inside my body, thrusting in and out in a perfect rhythm. Closing my eyes, I could feel it. My hands running over the glistening golden skin of his back as he gave me the most intense pleasure of my life, his eyes never leaving mine as he told me I was his forever.

"Aleria. Think of moldy bread. Sour milk. Gods help me, anything to calm down the lust blazing inside you. Damn it, I wish I had a sister right now." He muttered the last sentence, but the words were enough to break me out of my lust filled spell, like pouring a bucket of ice over my head.

Sariah.

My mission.

My breathing slowed as I settled calmly into his arms, falling back into my memories of my sister. I would do this for her. I had to. It was life or death and I had spent my whole life protecting her and I wasn't about to fail her now. Falling too far under this dragon's spell would spell disaster for me and mean the death of my sister.

eight

XANDER

TEARING open the door to my suite, I swiftly placed Aleria in a chair and moved to the other end of the room. I needed distance from her before I kissed her again. I was such an idiot, kissing her in the first place. Black Dragon matings were fierce, beginning with a kiss from the male, which would secrete a hormone that caused the female to go into heat. Typically, it took several days, but it seemed the human system metabolized the hormone faster than a dragon would and Aleria was already fully under the spell.

Her cheeks were flushed and her eyes unfocused as she clenched her thighs together. I could almost read the thoughts that were running through her mind. They were the same thoughts that were running through mine. Us, entwined together, my cock ramming into her soft heat, my hands roaming her body, my tongue exploring every curve she possessed.

"Damn it," I cursed, running my hands through my hair. My body raged, my dragon roaring at me from within to take its mate. But I couldn't do that. Not without explaining everything to Aleria. She deserved that.

"Aleria."

Her gorgeous emerald eyes turned up toward me, her perfect white teeth nibbling on her lip, causing a growl to rumble in my chest. I wanted to replace her teeth with mine.

"Xander, what is going on?" She shuddered, her whole body shaking as she wrapped her arms around her middle to try and ease the ache I knew she felt inside.

"Aleria." I cupped my hands on her cheeks as I knelt before her. She leaned into my touch with a whimper. "You are my mate. One of the unique, shall I say... quirks... of a Black Dragon, is that when he finds a mate, he begins to secrete a special hormone meant only for her."

She narrowed her eyes at me, confusion marring her features. "You mean to say you basically poisoned me with some crazy dragon hormone?" Her voice rose in hysteria.

The smile quirked my lips before I could stop it. "It isn't something I can control. It's biology. As soon as midnight struck and I reached the age of maturity, the glands in my mouth began to produce the hormone. For you. My soul had already recognized you as my mate. My body has just caught up." I laid my forehead against hers, my heart racing inside my chest, afraid of her reaction. Of her possible rejection.

"So, what does this crazy hormone do? I am guessing it is the reason why it is taking every ounce of willpower I have not to tackle you and ride you until dawn?" She squeaked as the words left her mouth, as if she didn't believe she had actually said them, and I couldn't help the deep laugh that rumbled out of my chest. Her palm slapped over her mouth. She dropped her gaze from me, looking away shyly.

I ran my fingers through her hair, marveling at the texture. "You are utterly amazing," I breathed, rubbing a strand of hair between my thumb and index fingers. "I shouldn't have kissed you. This is all my fault," I whispered, guilt making my words heavy. Sitting back on my haunches, I looked up at her.

"My mate, I pledge myself to you. My honor is yours. My body, my soul, my sword is yours for as long as we may grace this world." I bowed my head, taking her small hand between my large ones, laying my forehead against her fingers. The ritual pledge was sacred between a Dragonkyn and his mate, made before the first joining where the male laid out himself for his female.

She gasped and pulled her hand away from me, whirling to her feet so fast the chair fell backward, crashing to the ground. "No, Xander. I'm not ready for this." Her eyelids fluttered shut, a tear leaking out the corner of each eye.

"Aleria," I said firmly. "This is not something that I was ready for either, but we cannot fight our fate, little one." My palms cupped her cheeks, thumbs swiping away the drops of moisture leaking down her face.

"But you are a dragon. You have had years to get used to this. I barely know you. I- I—" She hesitated, wrenching from my touch and turning toward the door. She was trying to leave.

My mate was rejecting me again.

The deep roar that echoed through the room had

her tripping over her own feet as she backed away further in fear. "This is not something that we can control! There are no other Black Dragons. My father, brother, and I are it. The hormone wasn't supposed to react within you so quickly. I have no clue what it will do to your body if it is left unchecked!"

Her chin lifted, even as her bottom lip trembled. "Why did you have to do this to me, Xander?"

The words tore at my heart. "*Rashka*." Never did I think I would utter the term of endearment. The word had no translation in English. In my native tongue it was the highest form of address for one's mate. The unlimited term of love and devotion. This beautiful human had affected my body so much, in just a matter of hours, that I uttered the word desperately.

I was a Black Dragon Prince. I never begged, I never pleaded. But I would do it all for this fierce woman fighting through her tears, through the haze of arousal I knew had to be overwhelming her, as it was beginning to overwhelm me.

The soft moan that left her throat at the word almost took the breath out of my lungs, and when she whispered my name, I descended upon her, slamming my lips over hers, unable to hold back any longer.

"*Rashka*." I kept uttering between kisses, my tongue invading her mouth, sliding along hers. I felt her soft hands dig into the flesh of my neck before tunneling into the strands of my hair. More of the sweet secretions pooled in my mouth, only to be swept up by her tongue, causing her to moan and grind her pelvis into mine.

"Xander. Please. I can't think. It hurts." Her teeth sunk into my bottom lip and the metallic tang of blood filled my mouth, causing me to groan against her soft lips.

"I'll take care of you, baby." My lips trailed down her neck, nibbling and leaving my mark upon her skin. Dragons could be possessive creatures and I needed everyone to know this woman belonged to me. "Trust me." Sliding the straps of her dress down her arms, the fabric slid down to the floor.

She stood before me, wearing only a lacy strapless bra and matching panties, and leaning back, my mouth fell open as I took in her beautiful curves. "You are absolute perfection." The flush that colored her cheeks deepened and spread throughout her whole body. "And you are all mine."

My palms slid from her waist to her full ass,

pulling her body flush against mine. My erection dug into the soft skin of her belly as I flexed my hips forward. The little sounds that came from her throat left me hungry for more. I wanted to hear her scream my name as she came apart in my arms.

Her skin was so soft as I slid my fingers over her belly, to the tops of her panties. Her breath came in soft pants as my tongue traced a line along the tops of her breasts. "I love how soft your skin is." I closed my mouth over her nipple, through the fabric of her bra, her back arching into my touch, her eager hands reaching behind her back to unclasp the black material.

I chuckled, looking up at her through my lashes. "My mate is a bit impatient I see."

"Xander, everything hurts. I'm on fire," she groaned as my teeth bit down on the erect bud, pinching it then soothing the ache with my tongue.

"I know." I licked a long line over her sternum to the other breast, paying it the same attention. "So am I." To accent my point, I grabbed her hand in mine and led it to the front of my trousers, wanting her to feel how hard I was for her.

"Fuck," I cursed as she wrapped her hand around my shaft through the fabric. My eyes rolled back into my skull as she squeezed me. Her other hand fumbled with the buttons of my shirt. If she kept touching me like this, even through my pants, I was going to come like a teenager. She was wreaking havoc on my body. I needed this woman with every fiber of my being.

Securing her wrists, I stopped her stroking, giving me back a measure of my sanity which caused her to pout. I tore at the buttons of my shirt, sending them scattering to the floor with a pitter-patter as they rolled throughout the room. Next, I worked on the buckle of my belt, sliding the soft leather through the loops and discarding it on the floor next to the shirt, before unbuttoning the slacks and sliding them down. When I was standing before her in just my boxer briefs, her eyes smoldered as she looked at my body.

Aleria was nibbling on her lip again, eyes lingering on my defined chest and abs before flickering downward hesitantly. "Xander, I, uh," she stammered, "I need to tell you something."

I took her hand in mine, placing it against the skin of my chest, my lips returning to her neck. "What is it, little one?" The flush on her body deepened, her cheeks going cherry red, and she looked away from me.

"I, uh, am," those damn teeth were nibbling on

her lip again. Oh, the things that did to me. "I have never, uh, been with someone like you before." Her fingers curled on my chest, sliding down to the top of my abs, nails grazing my flesh.

I cocked my head at her. What was she talking about? "Aleria, what do you mean? A dragon? I would hope not," I huffed, frustration peaking within me that she would even bring up such a topic.

"Anyone. I haven't been with anyone before." The words were rushed out in one breath, mumbled together and so soft I could barely understand them.

Disbelief at what she said caused me to laugh, tilting her chin up to have her eyes meet mine. Tears shimmered in their depths. My laughter had hurt her; she was telling the truth. "You're a virgin?" The words were soft, my thumb brushing lightly over her bottom lip.

She nodded, trying to turn her head away in shame, speaking softly. "From the moment I first saw you, something inside of me sparked, and feelings that I had never felt before came roaring to life. Every time I saw you on TV, my gut would clench, but seeing you in person, it felt like someone sucker punched me." Her voice was thick with raw emotions.

Her words left me reeling. I took a step back, trying to cool the fire within my soul, trying to slow down so I could give my mate everything she deserved and more.

A virgin.

I would be her first and only.

The thought was intoxicating to me. My dragon roared in triumph, celebrating our mate and the pleasure we would bring her this night.

I breathed her name as I brought my lips back down to hers, kissing her gently, slowly, savoring the moment. Savoring each sound that she made, the way that her hands slid up my arms and down my back. "I'll go slow, baby." I breathed against her lips.

"I don't want slow, Xander. I told you that so that I wouldn't be lying to you." She winced as soon as the words left her lips, but she covered it up quickly as she kissed me again. Her arms wound around my neck as she lifted her body and wrapped her legs around my waist, bringing her center in line with my hard cock. Even through two layers of clothing I could feel her heat, her wetness, how ready she was for me.

I palmed her ass, walking toward my bed. I was going to lay claim to my mate.

nine

HIS STRONG HANDS gripped me firmly, his lips never leaving mine as he guided us toward what I assumed was his bedroom. A million thoughts tried to run through my head, but none could penetrate the haze of desire that I was feeling. The hormone or whatever it was that Xander had spoken of was something. It drove me wild, lowered all my inhibitions while making my body burn for him. I could feel the dampness of my panties between my thighs, my nipples hard and erect against his bare chest.

My back hit the soft mattress. My eyes were drawn to Xander as he stood over me, his body utter perfection as he crawled over me. My arms and legs opened to him, his weight settling on top of me as he gripped my hips to remove my underwear. I heard his harsh growl as his fingers parted my soft folds, feeling my wetness. His thumb circled my sensitive nub as the tips of his fingers teased my entrance.

"Baby, you are so fucking wet." His words were harsh, sending another wave of arousal through me. I loved his voice. I arched my back on a gasp as one of his large fingers entered me, giving my body time to adjust before circling lightly, thrusting in and out.

"And so tight." Xander's jaw was clenched, making the veins in his neck bulge. Another loud moan escaped me as a second finger joined the first, my hands digging into the soft fabric of the comforter beneath me.

"Xander, please," I moaned. His jaw released as he looked down at me, morphing into a devilish smile, his eyes glowing brightly in the dim light. His thumb brushed over my clit again, circling, drawing out my pleasure as his fingers continued to thrust in and out to the opposite rhythm.

"That's it, Aleria." The spasms started deep in my belly, my mouth opening on a silent scream. "Come for me." Spine arched, my entire body seized up as wave after wave of pleasure washed over me. His hands never stopped their ministrations, ringing every ounce of pleasure I had out of my orgasm.

Lips crashed over mine, swallowing my final cries as the last aftershock swept over me. Xander took his place between my splayed thighs, having removed his boxers. I bit my lip as I caught sight of his large cock. "Xander," I hesitated.

He smirked, kissing me again. "We'll go slow." He took his erection in hand, dragging the head through my slick folds, teasing my clit as I shuddered. An elbow planted next to my head, he leaned more of his weight down on me as he slowly entered my center.

My walls stretched, burning as he slowly sank his way inside. "You okay?" he breathed, his forehead against mine. At my nod of agreement, his hips drew back then forward, sinking in another inch. My hips arched into his at the feeling of fullness he was already creating within me.

"More, Xander. I need more." My nails clawed at his back, the burn within me climbing higher as he penetrated me further. With a final shallow thrust, he was fully buried inside me and held still, allowing me to adjust to his length and girth. His fingers clutched my hair, dragging my head back and baring my neck for his mouth.

"Fucking perfect." His teeth bit deeply before releasing quickly, marking me, claiming me. I clenched my thighs around his hips, digging my heels into the muscles of his ass, arching my pelvis, trying to get him to move.

His answer was to chuckle softly against my skin before his length slipped almost completely out of me before slamming back inside. I screamed in response, clinging to his back, my nails scoring his skin so deeply I'm sure I was drawing blood. His pelvis kept a punishing rhythm, thrusting in rapid succession that had my eyes rolling into the back of my head from the sheer pleasure.

Reaching down between our sweat soaked bodies, his thumb found my clit, strumming it in time to his thrusts. My climax shot through me like lightning, his name leaving my mouth on a scream as my vision darkened. Xander slammed against my hips, his nails digging into the soft flesh of my waist as he climbed to his peak. A deafening roar echoed through the room as I felt his hot seed release inside me.

Our bodies continued to move, shifting slightly to the aftershocks as we kissed gently, sweetly in the wake of our frantic lovemaking. "My *Rashka*," he whispered as he swept the strands of damp hair from my brow. A shiver ran down my spine at the word. I didn't know what it meant, but every time he had said it, my heart melted.

"Xander," I replied as my lips met his, our tongues softly mating, lazily exploring each other's mouths. I winced as he pulled his still semi hard cock from my body, before he rolled to his back, taking me with him and tucking me against his side.

"Are you okay, *Rashka*?" he asked, tilting my chin up, thumb stroking softly over my cheekbone.

A lazy smile spread over my face as I took inventory of my body. I was sure I would be sore soon, but for right now, I just felt deliciously sated and ready for sleep. Ready to escape the outside world and enjoy my time in the arms of my Dragon Prince. "Perfect," I sighed as I drifted off into a restful sleep.

Fire consumed me, swallowing me whole as I stared up into the flames coming out of the black dragon towering above me. Brilliant sapphire eyes I now knew intimately, narrowed at me as I burned, my screams echoing for a moment before ceasing abruptly.

"Aleria!" Xander shouted, shaking me awake, concern dripping from his tone. "Wake up, you were having a nightmare." He caressed my face as I blinked up at him, the scream of terror still lodged in my throat.

"Fire," I muttered, turning away from him, trying to pull away. "Burning." I probably wasn't making any sense to him, but my brain still hadn't fully grasped that it was awake yet.

Rays of sunlight filtered through the curtains, playing across my body. My eyes tried to adjust to the light. It was already morning? My arms wrapped around my middle, trying to stop the crawling sensation on my skin. "Make it stop." I moaned in pain, my nails scratching at my flesh.

Xander's eyes went wide as he looked down at me, securing my wrists beneath his. "Stop, Aleria. You're hurting yourself. It was just a dream." His tone was soothing, penetrating through the fog within.

I blinked as awareness washed over me, the strange sensation traveling along my skin torturing me. "Xander, my skin. It burns!" I bit out, fighting his hold.

"It might be a side effect of the hormone," he confessed. "I don't know. Damn it." He roared, the sound so fierce and loud that the pictures on the walls rattled with the force of it. His face was contorted with rage and a mixture of concern as he looked over me.

"Sh-Shower?" Now my teeth were chattering. It was like the night before, but this time there was no deep-seated arousal behind it. He gathered me into his arms, his skin against mine easing the stinging sensation. I rubbed against him seeking relief from the discomfort.

"Touching you helps." I brushed my cheek against his neck, my chest against his, sighing in contentment. The warmth of his bare golden skin under my fingers made my heart beat faster, but soothed the ache.

"It has to be the bond," he muttered, shuffling me in his hold as he adjusted the taps for the walk-in shower. I yelped as the water cascaded across my skin, before the temperature heated and the luke-warm water felt heavenly against my flushed skin. He placed me carefully along the tiled bench and knelt before me.

"I was able to call Drake through our telepathic connection. He should be here in a few minutes. We have to try and figure out what is causing this." His palms ran up and down my arms, spreading the warmth of the water along my skin. "Shit," he cursed, laying his forehead against mine as the shaking slowed. "I'm so sorry, little one."

"It's getting better." My fingertips grazed along the droplets covering his shoulders, fascinated by the path they were taking downward on his naked body. My tongue peaked out and traced a stray drop along his chin, causing a shudder to run through him.

"Tell me how you are feeling other than the shaking?" He pulled away slightly, separating our bodies and breaking the spell I was under. I blinked up at him, taking inventory of how I was physically feeling.

"Sore." My cheek pinkened, thinking of our activities last night and how wonderful he made me feel. "Muscles I didn't even know existed ache. I feel itchy, like something is trying to crawl out of my skin. I'm hot, but cold." Flicking my wet hair over my shoulder, I continued. "Being close to you helps."

He pulled down a bottle of shampoo and squirted a small dollop into his hand before massaging it into my scalp. I sighed, leaning back into his magic touch. "What was your nightmare about? Do you remember?" he asked gently, not pausing his ministrations. He pulled down a hand-held wand and carefully rinsed the suds from my hair.

I swallowed, hesitant to tell him. "A dragon burned me alive," I confessed, my voice a low whisper, barely heard over the sound of the shower.

"What?!" he roared again, making me wince at the anger in his voice.

"Xander, what the fuck is going on in there?" The voice I recognized as his twin brother echoed through the bathroom. Xander shielded me with his body, hissing as he stood in front of me.

"Drake, get out of the bathroom immediately," he bit out through clenched teeth. I heard Drake's answering laughter as he shut the door gently behind him.

Xander turned to face me again, taking my hand in his and laying it against his chest. "We are not done discussing this dream. Are you feeling well enough that you can finish showering on your own?"

I nodded in response. His lips parted in a small smile before he placed a gentle kiss on my forehead and departed the large shower stall. The breath I had been holding inside my lungs left in a loud exhale as I leaned my head against the cool tile wall.

ten

DRAKE ARCHED an elegant midnight brow at me as I departed the bathroom, a towel wrapped around my waist, my wet hair slicked back and water dripping down my back. He looked as if he wanted to start in on his teasing but was holding back purely based on the murderous expression I was sure I had on my face.

"Did you consult with *Pateros*?" I bit out, sweeping across the room to the closet to retrieve some clothing.

"I did, but he doesn't have a clue. Human physiology is so much different than our own, we may just have to wait and see. Although, we both agreed that a full physical and blood work should be done to ensure that she is healthy and there are no significant changes to her body."

Slipping on shorts and a tee shirt, I rubbed my hand across my face as I thought over his words. "Damn it, Drake. I didn't even think when I kissed her. It was pure instinct." To be honest, I wasn't sure I would have been able to resist the urge. She was too tempting, too beautiful, too perfectly mine.

His eyes shimmered as he looked at me, the pity evident, but underneath it was a hint of jealousy. Every dragon dreamed of meeting their mates as soon as they reached maturity. Existence could be lonely without the other half of your soul. "I know, Xander. I felt it through you. There was nothing more you could have done." He laid a hand on my shoulder in a gesture of comfort. "You tried to run away, but we had to call you back."

"Do you think the hormone will have a damaging or lasting effect on her? Honestly, Drake?" My voice was hollow, my mind going to all sorts of crazy scenarios that involved Aleria dying because she was my dragon mate. I would never be able to live with myself if I caused her any harm, even indirectly. I hardly knew her, but yet our souls were already connected on such a deep level.

Drake shook his head in response. "The humans

are compatible with us on every level. I can't imagine that there would be such an issue that it would cause any damage." He sighed, kicking out a chair before sitting down heavily. "We are the last of the Black Dragonkyn," he said, stating the obvious, but trying to lead me somewhere.

"Your point?"

He chuckled. "Biology may be accelerating matters within her body to prepare her to produce your children," he pointed out. Damn Drake and his scientific mind. Outwardly he may be a sarcastic asshole, but he had genius level intelligence.

Even though we were only fifteen when we arrived on Earth, we immediately began to study culture, sociology, science and medicine. Drake gravitated toward the latter two, and within the ten short years had grown to be one of our top scientists despite our age.

"There is no way in hell that is going to happen!" Aleria shrieked, stepping out of the bathroom, the towel wrapped tightly around her shapely body. Her face bore a mask of fury and anger.

Drake leveled a withering look at her. "You may have no choice in the matter, dear sister. The hormone running through your system may spur your reproductive cycle and drive you into heat. You will remain in a constant state of pain and arousal until you are impregnated." His words were said in complete confidence, without regard to her swirling emotions.

"No, I refuse to believe that." She held her chin high even as I saw the tears that formed in her eyes.

"We need to do further tests, sister. I think it best you don't have any physical contact until we know the results." Drake said, his face a grim mask.

I hated that he had to say the words, but until we had a better idea of what we were working with, they were necessary. He was right, although I wasn't going to admit it out loud.

She nodded. "I need some clothes, please," she said softly, her gaze not meeting mine, still glued to the floor. Her jaw was clenched tightly along with her fists, her expressive face not holding back any of her emotions.

"Of course," I nodded at her, retrieving a pair of shorts with drawstrings I knew she could tie to fit as well as one of my tighter shirts. The thought of her in my clothes made every possessive fiber of my being catch fire at the thought. Her eyes still refused to meet mine as she snatched the clothes from my hand and retreated to the bathroom, slamming the door behind her.

"So, brother, you seem to be handling this well." Drake covered his mouth with his palm to stifle the laughter that threatened to leave him.

"Sod off, this is your fault," I grumbled. If he had been a little more delicate with his theories, maybe she wouldn't be freaking out right now.

"Have her in my lab in thirty minutes and we can get started with the tests." I nodded in approval and Drake left quietly.

Sucking a harsh breath into my lungs and exhaling deeply, I knocked softly on the door. "Aleria, can I please come in?" I said, my voice low and soothing.

"No." The muffled response tore at my heart. My dragon wanted to roar and tear down the door.

"We need to talk, please. Can I come in or will you come out?" I laid my forehead against dark wood of the door.

My hands clenched into fists as her muted sniffles hit my ears, followed by haste shuffling around in the cabinets. Damn, I was really messing all of this up. I stepped back as I felt the handle move. Looking down at her red rimmed eyes I felt the pain radiating from her aura and my heart seized in my chest.

I gathered her into my arms without thinking of

the consequences, trying to soothe her with my touch. It seemed like the most natural thing in the world to do. "Drake said we shouldn't be touching," she whispered, her hands clinging to the cotton fabric of my shirt, contradicting the words she just uttered.

"Drake likes the sound of his own voice, so he talks constantly. Pay him no mind, I never do." I rubbed my chin on the top of her head, savoring the feel of her in my arms. "Are you feeling okay?"

"Yes," she said simply.

"I'll need a little more than that, sweetheart." I took a step back and lifted her chin up with my thumb and forefinger, making her gaze meet mine.

She gasped, seeing the intensity in my eyes, and expanded upon her answer. "The burning and tingling sensations have stopped. I'm not quite so sore and I don't feel like I am going to tackle you, so I think that is a vast improvement."

Oh, this woman and her wit. I laughed deep in my belly, my thumb lingering on her cheek before fully disengaging myself from her. My expression turned serious as I began to speak. "Aleria, I am not going to apologize for claiming you as my mate because I wouldn't be being honest. I will apologize for the manner in which I did so, though. You should have had a choice. I took that away from you."

Aleria just gaped at me, her mouth hanging open as I said the words. "Well, I guess that is better than nothing," she muttered, wrapping her arms around her middle.

"I value honesty above all else, Aleria. I will always be truthful with you, even if I know it is something that may displease you." It was a Dragonkyn principle, a matter of honor. We must be honest and trustworthy to each other in order to make our society work amongst the humans.

She blanched, her face drained completely of blood and she looked as if she was about to collapse. "Are you okay, what happened?" Concern dripped from my tone as I made a move to grab her.

A raised hand and shaking head stopped me before I could touch her. "No, I'm fine. It was nothing." Her voice was hoarse, the words dragged out of her throat with considerable effort. "Let's go see Drake so we can see what is going on with me."

ALERIA

When he uttered those words, my heart shattered. How was he going to react when he found out who my family was? I wasn't going to be able to keep the secret from him for very long, but I had to keep firm on my path to save Sariah. My sister was everything. Yet, why did the thought of that leave me in such shambles?

What was going to happen to me once I retrieved this silly artifact and gave it to my father and uncle? I knew Dragonkyn matings were for life, but what happens when one partner wanted out?

That was a ludicrous notion; matings were fated and no one wanted out.

Xander would surely want out once he found out what I had to do and who my family was.

My body had finally settled down, my heart rate returning to normal, and my skin no longer felt as if a million insects were biting me. The memories of the dream still haunted me and Xander's reaction was troubling. I hardly knew the man, but already I was so in sync with him. Of course, I had known all about Dragonkyn matings from the TV shows, but they had never spoken of them having this level of intensity so quickly. My soul yearned for him.

He led me out into the hallway, making sure our bodies didn't touch. The silence was deafening. I took in my surroundings as we made our way through the house. To say that this was a mansion was putting it lightly. The Black Dragon King and Princes lived in a home that was designed with luxury in mind. The hallway had chair rail height wood paneling, crown molding and expensive paintings that were expertly hung on the wall with placards and lighting. There were busts of famous philosophers and poets, statues of Greek gods and goddesses.

"Your house is like a museum," I uttered in awe. Of course, I had come from a family of wealth and privilege, but this was beyond anything I had seen before.

He rolled his eyes. "It is all a status symbol. Drake and I hate it. Father says it is necessary to try and impress people, to seem like we fit in and belong, but it just seems fake to me," he said simply as he looked around the room, taking in the various expensive items, his lip curling in disgust.

"We discovered early on after we arrived here that humans believed royalty to behave in a certain way and in order to blend in, we had to assimilate to that behavior. Our people know our real intentions, but the house is merely one of those ways we present ourselves to the world."

I stopped and turned toward him, cocking an eyebrow with a hand on my hip, questioning him with my gaze. "What are you talking about?" His cryptic musings were confusing to me.

Xander laughed. "In Dragonkyn culture, while the Black dragons rule, we don't really view ourselves as superior in anyway. We share our wealth, food and shelter with all. The Black dragons have ruled simply because we have been the most powerful, in the best position to defend and support our people."

"Dragons really are too good to be true," I muttered under my breath, not believing what I was hearing. How was this all true, and how was it that none of us knew about this?

"What was that?" he smiled, knowingly

"Nothing," I grinned sweetly. "So, the palace, the fancy clothes, cars... it's all to impress us lowly humans?"

His smiled dropped as his eyes burned, searing into me. "You are anything but a lowly human, little mate. And if I wasn't forbidden from touching you right now, I would show you just how much you mean to me." He stepped closer, his breath tickling the nape of my neck, sending goosebumps down my arms.

"Besides, the cars, those are purely a selfish fascination." The devastating smile on his face made my cheeks flush with warmth, tingles of awareness swirling throughout my body. "We enjoy anything that goes fast and the Italians and Germans have developed some wonderful machines that I am utterly fascinated with. I will have to take you out along the coast very soon so that I can show you my favorite spots." His fingers grazed my cheek with the barest of touches.

I turned my face away from his, continuing our journey along the hall. He exhaled, frustrated that I pulled away from him.

"I know this all seems like a lot to you." His agitation was evident as he ran his hands through his wavy black hair. "Tell me about your family. Do you have any siblings?"

Closing my eyes, I slowly counted to ten, trying to decide what I was going to tell him. I was playing a very dangerous, deadly game with a dragon prince. *But he is your mate*, something inside of me whispered, trying to make me understand and see reason.

"I have a sister, Sariah. She is five years younger than me." I swallowed harshly before continuing. "She was born with a very rare genetic condition that weakens her immune system. Even the smallest cold virus can be devastating to her." I felt the tears shimmer in my eyes; I hated talking about this with others.

Xander tilted his head at me, surrounding me in the warmth of his sapphire gaze. "You care about her very much."

I just nodded. "She is everything to me. Our parents—" I hesitated, clearing my throat "—are not the most nurturing of people and if it wasn't for me, she wouldn't receive the care that she needs. I had to be the one to make sure that doctors' appointments were scheduled and that she was taken to them, to pick up her medication, get her diet correct, comfort her and take care of her when she did become sick."

Damn it, I needed to stop talking about this before I started sobbing. The subject of Sariah was the one thing that could bring me to tears this quickly. I didn't know if they would stick to their word and take care of Sariah while I was here. It had only been a day, but I already missed my sister. I desperately needed to talk to her about what was happening with Xander.

"That burden should not have been placed on you." His voice was barely more than a growl. "It is a parent's duty to care for and love their children, not place them in harm's way." The fierceness of his statement made me pause. His eyes glowed in the low light of the hall, his hands clenched into fists as he visibly struggled to contain his emotions.

"Yeah, my parents are not really the type for 'duty'." I laughed at the irony.

"I will be having words with them for putting my mate in such a position." His voice was low and menacing, leaving no doubts in my mind that he would confront my parents.

"No!" I shouted, scared to death of something happening to Xander at my parents or my uncle's hands. Stealing from him was one thing, but physical harm was another. Xander was much stronger and had his ability to shift on his side, but I knew that the Brotherhood had been developing poisons that prevented the Dragonkyn from shifting, thus making it much easier to overpower them if they had a group.

"No," I said, much softer this time. "I can't risk them doing anything to harm Sariah."

His response was a grunt as we made our way through another corridor. His mouth was set in a grim line, brow furrowed as he contemplated my statement. This room was in vast contrast to the previous ones. Stark white walls, the same solid wood door, but this one with an electronic lock and keypad next to it. Xander approached and slid his thumb over the pad, which illuminated green, and the door opened with a click.

"Welcome to my lab, little sister," Drake boomed, arms splayed open, a wide grin on his face.

eleven

XANDER

MY LITTLE MATE was hiding something about her family. Her story about her sister was sincere. Every word she uttered chipped away at my heart. Aleria was a fierce woman who protected her sister at her own personal cost, but why was it when I mentioned having a chat with her parents that she panicked? There was something there, and I would have to find out what.

Drake was showing Aleria around the lab, introducing her to his various scientific toys and gadgets, most of which I had no clue about.

"So, you haven't had anything to eat yet this morning, correct?" Drake asked, his eyes leveled at me. He gave me a shake via our mental bond, to get my attention.

Aleria shook her head as I cursed. Some mate I was, not even feeding my woman.

"In this case it is a good thing. Aleria, if you would please have a seat here," he indicated a chair next to his phlebotomy supplies and drew on nitrile gloves. "I will just have to get a few vials, shouldn't be too much. Do you have any trouble with needles?"

She shook her head, watching as Drake opened the blood draw kit. "Good," he commented, "I am also going to attach these to your temples to get a few readings of your brain waves. Nothing to be alarmed about, just standard stuff for us." The way he smiled at her made me curl my lip. Drake placed two electrodes to her forehead, taking great care not to make direct contact with her skin.

Moving onto the blood draw, he secured a blue rubber strap to her upper arm, then swiped at the crook of her elbow with an alcohol wipe before setting the butterfly needle in place. A slight wince was the only reaction from Aleria. The vials filled quickly, for which I was thankful because seeing my mate so close to my brother was making me feel very possessive. The sight of her blood didn't help any either.

"All set," Drake smiled and winked as he

wrapped a bandage around her arm after he pulled the needle from her skin. "I would probably suggest some food before we do the physical. The doctor is also taking her sweet time to get here this morning, so it gives you the opportunity." He pinched and removed the wires and sensors from her head as well.

"Monika?" I responded, curious when he said 'she.'

"Yes. I knew that it would be a very bad idea for me to perform the physical myself as I am sure your mating instincts are going off the charts right now with me even being this close to her."

Aleria snorted, rolling her emerald eyes at me. "What, Xander, are you jealous of your brother or something?"

Drake sobered, pinning her with a withering stare. "Aleria, this isn't a laughing matter. Dragons in the first stage of mating are extremely possessive beings. Having his mate be touched by another male during this time has led to more than one bloody fight. I have no desire to fight with my brother today. He is on edge enough with us just being in the same room together."

She blinked at him, before sliding her glance to me. "They really don't cover this in the TV shows."

My eyes collided with Drake's, our eyebrows arching before deep rolling laughter poured out of us. "Little mate, you really are a delight," I said, tears pooling in my eyes from the force of my humor. "The shows, which I produce and direct by the way, are never going to show that intensity of it. They show some possessiveness, which ladies like, but we do not want negative publicity out there for our people."

Everything had to be about image for us. As I had explained to Aleria earlier about our home, it was a status symbol, something that was expected of us as the Dragonkyn royalty. We had to keep up appearance to the humans. There were already a number of radicalists that called themselves the Brotherhood for a Pure Society who were causing problems for our kind. They had been responsible for various terrorist attacks against Dragonkyn, one of them even resulting in the loss of a male and his mate. The thought of their deaths made me furious, wanting the fiercest revenge that I could enact against them.

"You produce the shows?" She sounded surprised.

"Yes. We don't just sit in our ivory tower, watching Netflix all day. Drake is a brilliant scientist and in charge of all of our medical research, which includes working with your government to synthesize vaccines to diseases that Dragonkyn have long been immune to." Drake smirked at the praise, his ego not needing anymore inflation, but I had to show Aleria the good that we were doing for her world.

"I studied sociology, organizational, and regular psychology in addition to communications. I have been the CEO of the TV network for the past three years." While my work might not be as important as Drake's in the physical sense, I am responsible for the image of my people and how they are viewed by human society. It was vital to our survival to fit in and be well received by the humans, who, while technologically inferior in every way, could defeat us with their sheer numbers.

Aleria stared at us both with wide eyes, "Wow. Just wow." She rubbed at her face and turned toward the door. "I am seriously starving, Xander, can we please get some food before I pass out?" she whispered, desperation underlying in her voice. She was obviously deflecting, and I would indulge her in this instance.

Turning to Drake, who just shook his head and waved me off, I rolled my eyes in response and approached my mate. She was starving, over-whelmed and tired. I was doing a horrible job of caring for her. It was my duty as her mate to see to her every need. I caught the growl that threatened to leave my throat and held a hand out to lead her out of the lab.

"Aleria, I am sorry that I have not been a proper mate to you yet. I haven't even seen to your basic needs," I bit out through clenched teeth as we approached the kitchen. Her body language remained closed off, her arms wrapped around her middle, head tilted down and eyes downcast while she stared at the floor.

She shook her head at my words as I held open the swinging door that led to the heart of the kitchens. It was late morning, the kitchen was done with preparing breakfast and not yet set to prepare lunch, so it was deserted. Instructing her to sit on one of the stools, I pulled out several containers from the fridge, thankful that there were usually leftovers hanging out that Hilde kept because either Drake, I or the staff would gobble them up.

"It looks like there is quiche, French toast, bacon, sausage and pancakes left. Any of that sound good?" Her emerald eyes caught mine, blinking at me in confusion as if she hadn't heard a word that I had said.

"What?" she asked absently, lost in her own thoughts.

"Aleria." I said, drawing her attention back to me. "You need to eat. What sounds good?" I held my arm out, indicating the different options that she had to choose from.

"Oh. Uh," she licked her lips, swallowing heavily while putting a hand over her belly. "French toast with bacon and sausage?" she said, her voice rose in a question. She still was too hesitant with me.

Nodding in acknowledgment, I pulled two plates out of the cabinet and piled the food up for each of us. A few minutes later, Aleria was digging into her butter-and-syrup-covered French Toast, the moan of approval leaving her throat had my cock hardening in my pants once again. Damn, this woman could set me on fire with just a sound.

"Thank you, Xander," she whispered, wiping her mouth with a napkin as she finished her plate of food. I inclined my head, picking up her plate along with mine and placing them both in the sink.

My hands firmly planted on the counter before the sink, I stood and hung my head low, eyes closed as I debated what to do next. I had been so used to my life going the way I had intended it to. On a planned path, one that I controlled. In one night, a small sprite of a woman came rushing in and threw everything off track.

"Xander?"

The hesitation and question in her voice had me gripping the counter so hard I felt the stone crack beneath my fingers. Forcing the calm into my voice, I addressed her without turning, not trusting myself to face her yet. My emotions bubbled just beneath the surface, with my dragon so close that my features would be heavily distorted. "Yes, little one?"

"Do you know where my phone is? My sister is probably worried that I haven't checked in with her yet and since I was gone all night..."

The smile spread across my face before I could stop it, thinking of the beauty of our mating last night. "It is probably upstairs in my room. I had your belongings gathered and put there. Let's make sure that Sariah is not concerned about your wellbeing before the doctor arrives."

Aleria hesitated, confusion flashing across her face as I turned to stand before her. "Xander, is all of this necessary?" she gasped. "I mean, I am human, how are you even sure I'm your mate?" The self-doubt in her words made me growl.

My palms cupped her cheeks, tilting her head up toward me. "Aleria, you are, without a shred of doubt, my one true mate. Human or not, it does not matter, you are it for me. If you don't feel the same, you can walk away. It may kill me, but I would let you go if that is what you truly want."

I didn't want to say the words but felt in my heart that Aleria needed me to say them in this moment. I could only imagine how she was feeling. Trapped, scared and alone, feeling things that she possibly and hopefully had never felt before. Her swift intake of breath as the last sentence left my mouth, followed by her rapid heartbeat made my heart break. Was this going to be the moment she was going to run away from me?

No, my stubborn little mate had other plans. She rose to the tips of her toes and laid a soft kiss against my lips, careful not to press too hard. "Xander, I can't deny that I am terrified of what is happening or how this is going to play out, but I also can't deny that what I am feeling is real. The thought of leaving you makes my heart ache and air leave the room." She shook her head. "So, no, I won't be leaving just yet. I appreciate the offer, though."

She dropped back down to the flats of her feet, staring up at me with her intense emerald gaze.

"Can we go get my phone now so I can check in with Sariah? I need to make sure she received her medication this morning."

"Of course." I nodded and led her out of the kitchen with a firm hand at the small of her back.

She never saw the small smile of triumph that lingered on my face.

twelve

XANDER'S WORDS, offering me a way out, lingered in my mind as we made our way back upstairs to retrieve my phone. Would he actually let me go if I were to just walk away now? No, that wasn't even an option. I had to retrieve the stupid artifact that my uncle needed so that Sariah would stay safe. I had no other choice in the matter. My heart shuttered at the thoughts and I quickly shut down the line of questioning.

His hand was firm and warm at my back, obviously ignoring Drake's warning of refraining from touching me. It was comforting, his touch soothing me in ways that I couldn't yet fathom. "Tell me about your family. I know about your brother, and a little about your father, but what about your mother?" I knew it was a deeply personal question, one that he probably didn't want to talk much about considering his mother died when he was an early teen, but I needed to know more about this male that was my mate.

I felt his fingers clench as his eyes took on a faraway look. "She was one of the most beautiful dragons ever born. From a blue dragon family that lived high up in the mountains of our home world. She used to tell me stories of how cold the winters were, the snow building up taller than their homes. My father came through on an outreach expedition, shortly after he took over the throne when my grandfather died."

The smile on his face was enchanting as I hung on his every word. "He said the second he saw her, he leaped from his horse, took her into his arms, shifted into his dragon form and flew away with her. They were secluded for weeks as they sealed their mating. It was a grand tale back home, an inspiring story after the tragedy of my grandfather's death."

"Of course, my mother had a bit of a different version," Xander chuckled. "She said that Father was a brute, picked her up without saying one word to her, and dragged her away. They loved to tease each other as they would tell the story over and over again." He paused, pain clouding his features as he briefly closed his eyes.

"Drake and I hated the story, we would groan and complain every time they brought it up, but now, we would both do anything to hear them tell it together just one more time."

Tears filled my eyes as I laid my hand against his cheek, my head leaning down to his strong chest as he gathered me into his arms. "What did she look like?" I asked, softly, curious about the woman who he spoke of so lovingly.

"She had hair so blonde it was almost white, and piercing ice blue eyes. One look at her and you could mistake her for being soft and frail, but one wrong move or misstep and she would put you back in place so fiercely your head would spin. She was a fierce dragon, loyal and protective of her family and clan. I swear she had eyes in the back of her head too." He shook his head, laughing quietly. "She had to, Drake and I were not the best of children."

I chuckled. "Somehow, I can imagine that. You two had to be a serious handful." Another devastating grin had me biting my lip.

His expression turned grim as his continued. "When the disasters started happening, she insisted on staying through the worst of it. Always said it was her duty as queen to help her people. She became ill shortly after a volcanic eruption, her lungs were singed from the hot air and ash she breathed in. Even her dragon healing could not aid her. It was already too far gone. We couldn't believe it, a dragon being burned by fire."

His eyes glistened with tears. "We could do nothing but make her comfortable as we sat by her bed and watched her fade into the next life." He paused, swallowing deeply, composing himself. "I didn't think my father would recover from his grief, but he knew he had a duty to his people to move forward. Drake and I were too young to help him with the responsibilities of the crown, so he had no one to shoulder the burden with any longer."

"He became obsessed with finding another planet capable of supporting our people as the prognosis of our home world stated we only had a few short months before total collapse. Once Earth was found, we were all gathered up and made our way here." He pressed a kiss to the crown of my head before opening the door to his suite of rooms.

"Thank you for sharing that with me Xander." I wrapped my arms around his waist and squeezed tightly before letting him go. I immediately regretted the loss of his body against mine.

"We are getting to know each other, little one." He tucked a wisp of hair behind my ear, his eyes still haunted by the memories of his past. "It is customary to share the stories of our past."

"I know but, still, thank you," I whispered, placing my fingertips on his lips, wishing I could kiss him properly. But, until we knew how the hormone would continue to affect me, no more kisses from my handsome dragon mate.

"Call your sister, Aleria, ensure her that you are safe." He smiled down at me, his soft blue eyes captivating me with their warmth and emotion. He retrieved a bag from the corner of the room which held my dress, under garments and my small clutch inside, handing it to me before retreating to the other room to give me some privacy.

Exhaling sharply, I sat down heavily on the sofa in the living room, staring down at the dozens of notifications on my phone. Luckily, the phone was still at twenty percent battery, leaving me enough to get through the notifications and contact Sariah.

I went through the texts first. Sariah had dropped a few in the beginning of the evening saying that she loved me, that she hoped I would have a good time and that I would meet some handsome dragons. Then there were harsh texts from my father and uncle.

> Uncle: You better not have run. You know we will let your whelp of a sister die if you run away from your mission.

> Father: You dirty whore, out all night. Alright getting right down to business I see.

> Uncle: You work quickly. Already have one of them in your bed? Or maybe you have both. No matter, you will do what we want you to do.

> Father: Stupid filthy cunt. You are no daughter of mine. Soiling yourself with dragons.

> Uncle: I see the dumb brutes couldn't resist your charms. Report back to the house by 3pm for your next steps or we will withhold all of Sariah's medications from her.

Angry tears fell from my eyes as I read the messages. Conflict raged within me. Lost in my thoughts, I jumped when the phone began to buzz in my hands. Sariah's name flashed across the screen and I sighed in relief.

"Monkey, are you alright? Have they hurt you?" My voice was desperate, frantic.

"I'm fine, Aleria." She was weak.

"Sariah, did they give you your medication this morning? Or anything to eat?"

She just sighed through the phone, "It seems they forgot about me again." A small, weak laugh echoed through my ear. "Tell me about the party. You didn't come home, so that must mean something happened."

"Sariah, listen to me right now. I am going to call Father. You need to take your medication and eat or else you won't recover properly from this little cough you have." Damn them. I was going to kill them for this.

"Aleria, don't do this. Enjoy your mate." She sounded so weak, so fragile, but her words made me pause.

"Wait. How do you know he is my mate?" I asked breathlessly.

"It is all over the internet, Ria. There are pictures of you two out on the balcony. Him carrying you away from the party. The gossip sites are all in a flutter about it. I can hear father and uncle shouting up here."

My mouth fell open, the phone almost slipping from my hand. "Oh my god I'm so screwed," I muttered, putting my head in my hand. "Ari, I've got to go, but I'll make sure that someone brings you food and your meds. Please take them. I will be home as soon as I can."

She huffed at me before disconnecting the phone. My mind was whirling as I brought up my social media account and saw the numerous messages and tags from old acquaintances asking me about my relationship with the Dragonkyn prince.

"Shit, shit, shit," I repeated, thumbing through the dozens of articles that speculated and assumed that I was his chosen mate. Some were even predicting the arrival of a new dragon princeling in nine months' time.

I fired off a quick text to Lucille, our head house-keeper, asking her to sneak some food up to Sariah's room through the servant's staircase. Within the message I added our code that meant to grab her spare medication that I had stashed just along the exit of the corridor as well. She responded immediately with a thumbs up, and I exhaled sharply, relieved that one thing would be going right this morning.

The phone buzzed again, this time my Uncle's name flashing across. I buried my rage and answered the phone with a gruff "Yes?"

"Your job was to seduce them, not to fucking mate with one of them." He was furious. I could only imagine how red he was, sweat beaded along his brow and spit flying from his mouth as he uttered the words.

"I can't really control that, now can I?" I bit out sarcastically.

"Do you really think it wise to talk back to me, little girl? When your poor sister is in such a terrible predicament? What if we were to leave one of her bedroom windows open all night? Perhaps she would catch a terrible cold. Without her very expensive medical treatments, she would perish in no time, I am sure." I heard my father and mother in the background, their cold laughter all blending together.

"I'll find your stupid artifact. Just tell me what I'm looking for." My jaw ached from how hard I was clenching my teeth together. "But I won't give you a thing if you don't continue Sariah's treatments and feed her. Don't think I don't know that you left her to starve since I left." It was my only bargaining chip. My only hope was that they wanted this, whatever it was, so badly that they would keep up their end of the deal.

"We shall keep our end of the deal, you brat. But know that your little relationship now complicates matters. You will need to dispose of him if you want to see your sister again."

My heart slammed in my chest, stuttering as he said the words. "What do you mean?"

"Oh, silly girl, he will never let you go. You are going to have to kill him if you are going to get out of that house alive. I will send you a picture of what it is we are looking for. You have three days. If that key is not in my possession at the end of the third day, Sariah will be dead, and it will be all your fault."

The line clicked dead, the phone dropped from my hands as tears streamed down my face, the thought of having to harm Xander physically made me sick. I knew I could never hurt him, but I would have to be creative to get this key and get out of the mansion to rescue Sariah.

Why don't you just tell him everything? He has resources, he can rescue her and keep her safe from the family. The nagging little voice inside her head yelled at her to trust my mate with the truth, beg his forgiveness and help with my desperate situation.

No.

I would do this and then leave. He deserved a better mate than me, anyway.

thirteen

XANDER

PACING THE OTHER ROOM, I left my mate to tend to her affairs. It was extremely early in our relationship, so I needed to learn to give her space to do her own thing. As I picked up my own phone, my brow furrowed at the number of notifications I had, ranging from text messages, missed calls and voicemails.

A voicemail from my assistant, Ashley, had me pinching the bridge of my nose and growling. "Xander, what the fuck? You get a mate and you don't even call? We need to do a press release and damage control ASAP. You need to call me the second you get this!"

I was worried this was going to happen. I knew with the amount of press at the event last night, someone may have been able to snap a picture of Aleria and I at some point. Scrolling through my emails, I discovered it was just that. Several gossip magazines wrote articles detailing their version of the evening's events.

The curse that left my mouth was fierce and I even felt the smoke leave my nostrils as I pressed the call button to ring Ashley.

"Xander, fucking finally. What the hell is going on?" Her voice was frantic, an unusual sign from my always well put together and organized personal assistant.

"Well, Ashley, I think that would be rather obvious. I reached my maturity last night and found my mate." I chuckled, wishing it was as simple as that.

"Damn it, Xander, I am buried in requests for interviews, for photo ops, for any details on the mystery woman that they caught on camera as you carried her away." I heard her shuffling around papers followed by a deep sigh that ended on a groan.

"Are you at the office? I thought I told you specifically to take the damn weekend off?" I growled at her.

"How the hell can I do that when the social media world is blowing up around us because you found your freaking mate?" She blew a raspberry at me. "Congrats by the way," she followed up, quickly.

I shook my head and laughed softly. "Thanks, Ash. You'll like her. She has spunk and is full of sass. Let's just say that it has been a very interesting twenty-four hours." I ran my fingers through my hair in agitation, pacing the length of my home office.

"I'll do what I can to hold off the vultures but start thinking strategy on how we introduce her to the world, because they are dying to know more about her. See you on Tuesday."

I said my goodbyes and slid the phone back into my pocket. That was why I paid Ashley the big bucks. She was a human but had proved her loyalty time and time again. She was more than just my personal assistant, she really was more like my right-hand-man. In fact, she didn't know it yet, but I was already planning on giving her a sizable promotion to a new position that I had created as the Director of Community and Social Engagement. It was right up her alley and she more than deserved it. We always took care of our own, regardless if they were human or Dragonkyn.

My head cocked as a feeling of despair settled in my stomach.

Aleria.

There was something wrong.

I left my office and approached her in the living room, watching her quietly as tears streamed down her beautiful pale face. "Aleria, what happened?" Sitting down beside her on the couch, I gathered her in my arms. Her body shook with the deep sobs as she struggled to speak.

"Baby talk to me. Did your family say something awful? Is Sariah okay?" I wiped away the wetness on her face, my thumbs lingering and stroking a soft rhythm against the skin of her cheekbones.

She shook her head. "No, everything is fine. I had to contact my housekeeper to send her up some food because they forgot, but other than that she was okay." The smile that graced her face was forced, put there only for my benefit. More happened during her conversations than she was telling me. I would have to get Klaas to check into her family immediately to see what he could tell me about them. There was something that I couldn't quite put my finger on here.

"Why were you crying, *Rashka*?" I swept the hair from her face, placing a kiss against her forehead.

"Overwhelmed, tired, shocked." She swallowed, looking me squarely in the eyes, her gaze flickering with fire now, "Did you see the articles on the internet about us?"

Exhaling loudly, I nodded. "We are aware. My assistant is doing what she can to put out fires, but we will have to plan on a press conference or a released statement soon to keep the vultures off our backs." Her spine stiffened at my words, a shudder running through her small body.

"Xander, I need to—" Her comment was cut off by the shrill ringing of my phone.

"Drake," I answered, indicating to Aleria who it was on the other end.

"Monika has arrived and is on a bit of a tight schedule today. Can you please bring Aleria down as soon as possible?" Drake sounded off, but I wasn't going to question it while in my mate's presence. I had a feeling it had to do with her blood work results. I could sense his agitation through our bond.

"We'll be down shortly." I ended the call before I pulled the phone away from my ear.

"Let's go, little one." I rose to my feet and held out a hand to assist her up. "The doctor awaits."

She hesitated, wringing her hands together on her lap. "What is going to happen after the exam?"

I narrowed my eyes at her. "What do you mean?"

A deep sigh left her lips. "Xander, I mean, what happens? Where do we go from here? I need to go home and see my sister. I have a life."

Of course she did. She also needed to gather up her belongs because there was no way in hell that I would allow her or her sister to stay under that roof any longer than absolutely necessary. A growl left my throat at the thought.

I chose to calm my errant thoughts, not wanting to frighten her. "Let's take it one step at a time. Once we are done with the doctor, we can go to your house and get a few things for you to stay here for a few days? We will have to wait for the news to die down a bit before you can go about your normal routine, so staying here is the safest option for now."

She placed a hand on my chest and took a step back. "I am going to my house, alone. Not with you," she said firmly, her fist on her hip.

"Aleria, the reporters may not know who you are now, but they will find out. We have enemies, people who do not want Dragonkyn and humans being together." I held my ground. I would not leave my mate unprotected. Not when I had just found her.

"I know that," she grumbled under her breath.

I continued, "And my duty as your mate is to

protect you. I cannot let you go out alone right now. If you can't agree to my condition, then we can send someone over to your residence to grab some items and to check on Sariah for you. I would even send Drake for you if it would put your mind at ease having someone you know go."

"No!" She protested harshly. "No, you don't have to send Drake." She sighed. "What about your assistant? She is human, isn't she?"

My eyebrows arched as I regarded her. What did Ashley being a human have to do with if she could retrieve items from Aleria's house or not? This situation was growing stranger by the second.

"That is a good idea. I will reach out to Ashley and ask her to retrieve some items. If you get me a list, I'll send it to her." I nodded as we left my rooms, making a mental note to get Klaas investigating as soon as physically possible.

Drake greeted us with a smile that did not quite reach his eyes. Monika, our family's primary doctor for years, warmly introduced herself to Aleria and then escorted her into the exam room. I jerked my head to the side, indicating for Drake to join me in his office, which was sound proofed, ensuring we would not be overheard.

Holding up a hand to stop Drake I spoke. "Before you begin with what is bothering you, I need to make a call to Klaas. Now."

I pulled my phone out of my pocket and dialed his number. As always, he answered on the second ring with a deep, "My Prince."

"Klaas, I need you to begin a thorough background investigation of Aleria Mikkelsen immediately. There is something that is off about the information she is telling me. Her family seems very peculiar. They are hiding something. I need you to find it." Drake's brow furrowed as he looked at me, the shock etched across his face.

"Something struck me as odd as well, my Prince. Not about the girl herself, but the aura surrounding her," Klaas spoke, his deep voice thick with mystery. He was the Captain of our guard for many reasons, the first of which was his loyalty to our family, but coming in a close second was the fact that he possessed an uncanny second sight and affinity for sensing auras. A useful tool when trying to learn someone's intentions.

Klaas was a purple dragon, possessing strong telepathic, psychic and telekinetic abilities. He was raised alongside my father, and they were the best of friends. The man would willingly lay down his life for any member of my family without hesitation. There was no one else I could trust with this matter.

"I think it is her family. Begin with putting men on watching their movements. Focus on the sister, her name is Sariah. She is an innocent in all of this and may be being used as leverage for something." I rubbed my chin as I spoke.

"It will be done my Prince. I will be in touch shortly with my findings." Klaas, ever the efficient man, would get to the bottom of this situation quickly.

Drake whistled as he sat down in his desk chair. "Fate sure knows how to pick them, doesn't she?"

The laugh that bubbled from me held no mirth, only frustration. "So, lay it on me, brother. What more do you have to pile on to my already fucked up situation?"

He cleared his throat. "It isn't exactly bad, just strange." He pulled a file out from his drawer, examining the results again. "Some of her levels are going through the roof. I pulled her medical records from the online database of the clinic she attends and compared them. Her numbers and her results from this morning are aligning more with Dragonkyn results than any human results."

"What are you saying, Drake? That the hormone is messing with her body and what, turning her into a dragon? That is ridiculous!" I exclaimed, laughing at the thought.

He set down two pieces of paper in front of me. "Here are your bloodwork results from last week, very standard normal numbers across the board for a Dragonkyn, right?" He pointed to one chart with various lines and levels. "Now here are Aleria's results from this morning. Her levels are way higher than any human that I have ever seen and just below yours."

"Her brain functions are also off the chart, Xander, matching ours. The hormone is changing her body. I am guessing because nature has realized that we have no Dragonkyn females to carry on the black dragon line." Drake seemed utterly fascinated by it all, his eyes flowed over all of the data, a glimmer in their sapphire depths.

"Do you think this means that she will also have an increased immunity and life span?" I asked, sitting on the edge of my seat. It was one secret that we kept well hidden from the public. Dragonkyn lived for a lot longer than humans. My father was almost two hundred years old and still in top physical condition. Many of his men had shared this information with their mates, but the women seemed to be benefiting somewhat from their mate bond. Although the oldest couple had been bonded for just under ten years, Gregor's mate, Hillary had remained very healthy and had hardly aged in their time together. It was a test that only time would tell.

"I am almost positive if you remained physically intimate with her, that the benefits would remain." He grinned at me. "We all know that would not be any hardship." Clasping me on the shoulder, he sighed.

"The one thing that I am concerned about is fertility. Father has told us countless times how many miscarriages Mother had, and then how difficult her pregnancy with us was." The thought crossed my mind, making me dread the possibility of Aleria suffering the same fate.

"I know, Drake, but for now, we just have to do what we can. Do you think birth control will be effective on her?" I asked, knowing that neither of us would be ready for a child quite so soon.

"I believe so, Monika asked about it as well and said she would discuss it with Aleria during their exam. We both reviewed her results and concluded that the reaction that she had to the hormone could be controlled with a higher dose of a standard birth control shot."

"Good."

"Speak of the devil," Drake remarked as he saw Monika and Aleria walk back into the hallway. Aleria was smiling at the tall woman, she looked pleased with whatever they had discussed and at ease.

"Let me go get my mate," I growled, rising from my chair to take my place by Aleria's side.

fourteen

ALERIA

DRAKE AND XANDER APPROACHED US, Monika smiling as she reached out and gave each of the twins a firm hug and kiss. "Xander, you have got yourself one heck of a mate. Do not screw it up," she scolded him pushing her finger into his chest with narrowed eyes.

I turned a side gaze toward Drake and we both snickered at Xander's downcast look toward Dr. Monika. "Aleria, if you need anything, you call me okay? I gave you all my numbers on that card. If you feel any side effects from the shot, just let me know." She pulled me in for my own hug and I sighed in contentment at her motherly affection.

"I will, thank you for everything." Dr. Monika had proven to be just what I needed to settle my nerves through my young relationship with Xander. She had been around the twins since shortly after their arrival on Earth, became the family's personal physician, and saw to all of their healthcare needs. She understood the situation that I was being thrown into and tried to explain to me a little bit of what she saw was happening with my body.

"According to your blood results, the hormone is essentially making a more viable and healthier Dragonkyn mate. Your brain functions and vitamin levels are now just under those of a typical Dragonkyn female, suggesting that nature is trying to prepare you for future fertility and healthy children."

The words, while softly spoken, were blunt and matter of fact. Something that I appreciated, but I was still shocked at. Drake had theorized it, but now the blood and other scans had confirmed it. Yet, the good doctor had surprised me by continuing.

"We believe that a simple birth control shot will prevent pregnancy for now until you and Xander have that discussion about when you choose to bless us with little ones." Her smile was warm, easing my anxiety at the situation. I knew there would be no children, because once I got the key and delivered it to my Uncle, my life would be forfeit.

"It should also counteract some of the effects of the hormone, letting you both resume your exploration of your mating bond." She winked knowingly at me, sending heat flooding into my cheeks and turning them a shade of deep crimson.

After she finished the exam, she administered the shot before she escorted her back into the hall. The stories that Dr. Monika had shared with me of the twins as small boys had my belly still aching with laughter.

Xander turned toward me as Monika gathered her belongings and left the lab, making me grin wider. "You seem to have won her over, little mate." He smiled, sending a shiver of awareness running down my spine. That devastating smirk should be outlawed for what it did to me. "Not an easy thing to do with our tough-as-nails doctor."

Drake snorted. "Seriously. At times that woman is more of a dragon than we are." Xander and I both snickered in response.

"She was very nice to me. I have no idea why you would say that." I feigned shock at them. "Maybe because you two were such little hellions?" I added sweetly.

"You have no idea, darling," Xander whispered in my ear, before his teeth nibbled lightly.

"Oh, Xander, before I forget, *Pateros* said we are to all have dinner together. Six PM sharp as always," Drake said, looking down at his tablet, walking away to his research. "Until then, little sister." He winked at me, causing Xander to growl in response.

"See you then, brother," he bit out as he guided me from the room.

Xander guided me through the house, taking me on a tour through the various rooms of the vast mansion. "I am going to get very lost in this place," I giggled, then quickly sobered, realizing that I probably wouldn't be here for too long.

While we looked in the various rooms, I committed the layout to memory, analyzing it to refer back to later when I began my search for the artifact. Frustration rolled through me at the thought. I didn't want to do this, but I knew I must.

"Don't worry, you get used to it after a bit. It is laid out in a pattern. You just have to learn it."

As we were walking down the hall, we passed by a young blonde boy carrying a stack of paperwork, dressed in black slacks and crisp white shirt with a black tie. I cocked my head as his eyes met mine and a spark of recognition struck. I had seen this boy before. In my home, at a party.

What was he doing at Xander's house?

"How are you doing today, Daniel?" Xander asked the familiar stranger, his hand tightening on mine.

"I'm well, thank you, sir," the boy, Daniel, squeaked in response, a look of horror on his face as he looked at me.

"I must go, your father is expecting this file," he held up the bundle of papers he carried and darted through a door at the other end of the hall and out of sight.

That was strange.

"Daniel is a strange boy, but he is my father's valet slash errand boy, helping him out with simple tasks." Xander shook his head, rolling his eyes at the closed door that Daniel has walked through.

He turned to me and smiled with dark intentions before his lips descended on mine, backing me into the wall of the library.

"Aleria, I am dying for you," he whispered, his words husky as his lips hovered above mine. A firm hand slid along my leg, up to my thigh as I lifted and wrapped it firmly around his waist. "Are you dying for me too, little one?" Sharp teeth nibbled on my bottom lip.

His name was a plea as it left my throat, heat pooled between my thighs, sending waves of arousal throughout my body. He hadn't even properly kissed me yet, hadn't released his crazy dragon hormones into my bloodstream, yet, my body already cried out for his. "Kiss me," I uttered, twining my fingers through his hair and crushing my mouth to his.

Our tongues danced together, dueling as he thoroughly fucked my mouth. The tangy flavor that was purely Xander flooded my senses, drawing me under his spell, making me soft and pliant in his arms. His deft fingers slid up my waist, under my shirt to trace a line along the bottom of my breast, eliciting a shiver from me.

My other leg lifted from the ground as he fully supported my weight between the wall and his body. Hips arching into his, I ground against the firmness of his erection, moaning in delight at the friction along my aching clit.

"Xander, please," I whispered against his lips, my fingers working to slide down to the front of his pants.

He chuckled, pulling back to pull my shirt over

my head, followed by his. Xander was so impatient that, rather than set me back on my feet to pull down my shorts, he yanked the waistband and ripped them down the center. A groan rumbled from his chest as he realized I wasn't wearing any panties. He stroked my aching nub, making my back arch and a sound of pure need leave my throat.

"That's it, ride my hand." He bit down on the lobe of my ear as his hot breath washed over me. One long finger swept inside me, curling and stroking the inside of my channel. My hips bucked in response, the moans growing louder as he kept up a punishing rhythm. Rubbing lightly over my hard nub, he thrust two fingers deep at the same time he sank his teeth into the flesh of my neck.

The climax that washed over me left me breathless, floating on air as sensations flooded my body. His soft tongue soothed the ache from his teeth, his nose rubbing lightly over the mark as he withdrew his fingers from my body and settled the hand back on my hip. His firm cock nudged my slick folds, demanding entrance as his gaze collided with mine.

"Now, Xander." My nails dug into the flesh of his shoulder. My head snapped back in ecstasy as he seated himself inside with one deep thrust.

Soft words, whispered in another language

against the skin of my throat, left me panting as his cock claimed me. Every thrust, every sound of pleasure he uttered, heightened my pleasure, sending me into subspace.

His name was a chant on my lips as I reached another impossibly strong climax. His hand tightened on my hips in a bruising grip, his thrusts growing in their intensity as he reached his own peak on a long groan. "Aleria," he whispered, his lips moving over mine in featherlight kisses. Sweat beaded on both of our foreheads as he cupped my face in his large hands.

"*Rashka*"

The damned word again.

The tears gathered in my eyes, unbidden, and I tried in vain to swallow them down. A deep exhaustion settled in my bones as Xander set me back on my feet. A forceful yawn stretched my mouth as I fought the overwhelming fatigue.

He chuckled as he gathered me in his arms. I snuggled into his chest, asleep before we even got up to his rooms.

"Aleria," Xander said my name softly, his warm breath fanning over my neck as he traced my cheek with his fingertip. "Time to wake up."

I groaned as my eyelids fluttered open, gazing into his beautiful sapphire eyes as he beamed down at me. His head was propped up on one hand, braced on an elbow as his other still traced the line of my cheekbone. "You look beautiful, all sleepy and mused from my lovemaking," he rumbled as his thumb traced my lips.

A sound of pure need left my throat. "You know just what to say to a girl to make her feel special." My lips quirked in a half smile as I stretched out my aching limbs.

"I can make you feel special, all right, little one." He rolled on top of me, pinning my wrists beneath one of his large palms as my legs opened to wrap around his hips. His firm erection pressed into me, sliding along my folds, causing the ache for him to intensify.

I breathed his name, pleading for him to relieve the emptiness I felt inside of me. "We don't have time, little mate." He nipped my neck, as my back arched into him. "Dinner is in less than 45 minutes and we can't be late." He chuckled as he gracefully climbed to his feet, leaving me a throbbing mess on the bed. I eyed his naked backside hungrily as hc padded to the closet.

"Damn you, Xander." I muttered, sitting up and trying to tame my wild auburn hair back into some semblance of order. "I've known you a whole twenty-four hours and you are already driving me crazy." He just shook his head and chuckled.

"I wouldn't have it any other way." He leaned his head out of the doorway, winking before smiling at me. "Now get that adorable ass into the shower."

fifteen

XANDER

ALERIA EXITED the bathroom and lifted her eyes to me with hesitation. The air was immediately sucked out of the room as I took in her enchanting form, the dress that I had selected for her was perfect in every way. The emerald color brought out her eyes, the gold trim and accents reflected the highlights in her auburn hair, which was gathered atop her head in a simple knot. She was enchanting.

My mouth hovered open as she approached me, "Well? What do you think?" she asked, a coy smile on her face. Her eyes betrayed the tone as they looked for approval and praise.

I cupped her cheeks in my palms, tilting her head up toward mine as I kissed her lips softly. "You are the most beautiful woman I have ever laid eyes upon." I clasped her hand in mine, intertwining our fingers.

"Ready for dinner?" I asked.

She nodded, clearing her throat, blinking away the moisture in her eyes. "So, will this be super formal? Three different kinds of forks on the table type affair?" She smirked at me, trying to lighten the mood.

"Do you know the proper usage of each fork or do I need to give you a crash course?" I played along with her little façade as we left my rooms.

She chuckled, the light sound warming my soul. "Actually, I do. I was raised in an extremely formal, rigid household." The smile immediately left her face as an echo of a memory crossed over it.

I brought her hand to my lips, kissing the inside of her wrist before biting gently. "No, love. It's not a formal dinner. We typically have dinner together several times a week. With the hectic nature of our schedules, it is the one time that we have together as a family to simply enjoy each other's company. There tends to be a lot of business discussion, but Drake typically steers us in other directions and makes us laugh with his sarcastic wit."

She tilted her head up at me. "Do you always dress up for it?" She looked me up and down, eyeing my trousers, button down shirt and blazer. I had forgone a tie as I despised the things, only wearing them when absolutely necessary at the office.

"Father does like certain formalities, dressing semi formally being one of them." I leaned down and inhaled the skin of her neck, easing my nose along the dark smudges of a developing bruise where I had bitten her.

"Admiring your little love bites?" Aleria asked, quirking her brow at me. My answer was to place a lingering kiss along the mark and settle my hand at the small of her back. "Brute," I heard her mutter.

"I didn't hear you complaining when I gave them to you," I quipped, watching the flush rise up her cheeks.

"Ugh, you two are going to be insufferable, aren't you?" Drake made a gagging noise as he brushed past us, taking his seat at the dining table.

Aleria blanched before Drake winked at her, which I answered with a growl. "Stop flirting with my mate."

"Calm down, brother." He held his arms up in surrender. "I'm not flirting."

Aleria laid her hand on my chest, just above my heart. "Xander, he just winked at me. It was a joke. Nothing flirty or seductive about that," she murmured, rising on the tips of her toes to give me a soft kiss, calming my ire.

"Look at that, Aleria is a good ol' fashioned dragon tamer." Drake snorted as he laughed, slapping his hand on the table, making the wine glass in front of him rattle.

"Drakon, that is quite enough of that behavior!" Hilde scolded as she came out of the kitchen door, holding a bottle of wine in her hand. "We now have a lady in the house and you will be on your best behavior."

"Yes, Hilde," he grumbled, lowering his head like a child who got caught with their hand in the cookie jar.

Hilde's smile brightened as she settled her soft brown eyes on Aleria. Setting the bottle down on the table, she approached her, arms open wide, and engulfed her in a tight motherly hug. "My dear, it is so nice to meet you."

Hilde held tight to her hands, taking a step back to look at her. "Alexandros is a lucky, lucky dragon to get a mate so beautiful. You are too skinny though, we need to get some meat on your bones." She huffed and released Aleria's hands to begin pouring the wine.

The look on Aleria's face was priceless as she

stared at the short woman in her sixties. "Aleria, that is Hilde. She has been taking care of our household for many years. We would be utterly lost without her," I said, settling my hand across her shoulders, tucking a stray wisp of hair behind her ear.

"Darn right, young man. You two would never get fed or mind your manners," Hilde said gruffly, nodding her approval.

"Thank you for your kind words, Hilde," Aleria said, her voice low. My mate didn't know how to take compliments. With the little I knew of how she was raised, I wouldn't be surprised if she never received any in her short life.

"You are quite welcome, dear. Now sit, sit. King Dimitros should be here any moment." She waved her hand and indicated for them to sit in their usual spots.

"Thank you, Hilde." I kissed her on the cheek while pulling out the chair for Aleria to sit in. She was surprised at my gentlemanly gesture, but quickly smiled as I pushed her up to the table.

Drake was already drinking from his wine glass, so I pulled the glass to my lips as well. Aleria followed our lead and sipped as well. "Good wine selection, Hilde. What's for dinner?"

"Roast chicken, potatoes, spring vegetables and some fancy sauce that the chef came up with. He was very eager to impress your mate this evening." She beamed at Aleria again, stars in her eyes, as the blush crept up Aleria's face once again.

"You will have to get used to people wanting to impress you, my love. It is part of your world now," I smirked, winking at her shocked expression.

She swallowed, not looking up from her plate as she nodded. "I am not used to even being noticed, much less people trying to actually impress me. It is a lot to take in right now," she said, her voice soft.

I tried to respond, but my father chose that moment to walk through the door, causing the three of us to rise from our seats out of formality.

"Ah, Aleria, my child." His eyes sparkled in greeting as he took Aleria's hand and placed a gentle kiss across her knuckles. "It is good to see you again." He embraced her, his gesture one of fatherly affection. My heart beat faster in my chest. Seeing my mate be accepted by my father and king made my pride soar.

Dinner passed with ease, my father charming Aleria with his wit, and in return Aleria had my father wrapped around her little finger. His eyes kept meeting mine, as if to convey their approval of my mate, but there was something lingering behind the dark depths. I arched a brow at him to signal a question, but he brushed it off with a subtle shake of his head.

Shortly after we finished eating, Ashley arrived with the items requested from Aleria's residence. Klaas escorted her into the dining room as we rose to leave, both with severe expressions on their face, but wiped them clean when Aleria returned to us.

"Aleria, this is Ashley, my PA, and the brooding giant there is Klaas, the captain of our elite guard." Ashley plastered on a smile and reached out to shake her hand. Klaas said nothing, only nodded in her direction to acknowledge the greeting.

He must have found something very interesting in her background for him to act so coldly to her. He was a severe, quiet man, but never downright rude like this. The action was an obvious snub.

"Here are your things, Aleria. Your parents gave me quite a fit and wouldn't let me see Sariah as you requested, and then they wouldn't let me get a few of the items on your list." Ashley was flustered, with a fire in her eyes and redness in her cheeks. "I had printed the list so I circled those things, it's on top of the suitcase when you open it."

Aleria bristled, her back going stiff as she

listened to Ashley. "I'm sorry they gave you trouble. I appreciate you getting these for me." She turned, suitcase in hand and started walking up the stairs.

She paused, looking back at me. "Xander, I am exhausted, it is alright if I just go to bed now?" Eyes shining with moisture, Aleria's expression pleaded with me to let her have some time to herself.

Letting out a deep breath, I placed a gentle kiss on her forehead. "Are you alright getting back to our rooms on your own? I have a few items to discuss with Ashley and Klaas."

I watched, heart in my throat, as she nodded and walked away.

My head jerked in the direction of the study, making my way there with Ashley and Klaas close behind me. Pouring myself a drink, I closed my eyes and spoke, "Ashley, tell me what happened?"

She sighed, her arms crossed over her chest, her agitation had eased but she was still visibly upset. "Those people are monsters, Xander. You need to stay as far away from that girl as possible. There is no way that you can be around that evil without it rubbing off on you." She shuddered.

My anger rose, a growl rumbling in my chest. "What are you talking about? How are they evil?"

"There was an overwhelming feeling of evil in that entire house. The way they talked, the way they moved, the way they watched me. It scared me, Xander, and you know nothing really scares me other than spiders." Her breathing became heavy. Klaas settled an arm over her shoulder, providing her with a comforting touch. I could feel him pour some of his energy into the small human, feeding her positive emotions.

"Her uncle was the worst of all of them. He is a vile man. The way his eyes lingered on me. It made me sick." Klaas gathered her into a hug as the tears pooled in her eyes. Ashley was an extremely strong woman, but very susceptible to evil entities, making her the perfect judge of character. If she said that Aleria's family was evil, then evil they were.

The thought made me sick inside. I knew that Aleria was not like that, even if she had been raised by it. I had seen into her soul, seen her light. She wasn't like that, was she? Was I blinded by the bond somehow?

"Ash, I am very sorry that you had to go through that," I said softly as she sniffled into Klaas's black shirt.

"Please, Xander, I care too much about you to see you get hurt. You need to push her away," Ashley pleaded with me, her eyes wild.

I shook my head with regret. "It is too late for that, Ash. She is my mate, there is nothing that I can do." I paused. "She isn't like them, she isn't evil," I muttered under my breath, knowing in my heart that what I said was the truth. My dragon would not accept such a mate for us.

"Ashley, love, why don't you go see Drake and have him give you something to help you sleep tonight? Take one of the guest rooms on the west side of the house," Klaas said thoughtfully.

She nodded in response, giving him a small smile of thanks before leaving us in the study.

I poured another drink, holding up a glass to Klaas, offering him one as well. He took it with a grateful bow of his head. "So, I am sure you have even more to add to that lovely conversation." Sarcasm dripped from my words.

Klaas exhaled. "I'm afraid so, My Prince." He knocked back the amber liquid, handing the glass back to me for a refill. "From the intelligence I have gathered, it is looking like her uncle and father may be high level members of the Brotherhood."

The glass shattered in my hand, blood mingling

with the alcohol as it dripped down my fingers to the floor as I cursed. "Do you think she is involved as well?" I snagged a towel from beneath the wet bar and picked the glass out of my flesh.

"I don't believe so, but I also don't think it was a coincidence that she was at the ball yesterday either." Klaas crossed his arms over his wide chest and pinned me with a stare. "You do need to tread carefully, My Prince. You may be mated, but that does not mean that she won't betray you. There is something that she is hiding and it has to do with her family, I am sure of it."

"What about her sister? Did she lie to me about that?" I asked through gritted teeth.

Klaas shook his head, his look turning to one of pity. "Unfortunately, that is completely true. The girl has been seriously ill most of her life. The medical records are extensive. The worst part of it all is that the parents don't seem to care about her at all." He growled in disgust. Our honor as Dragonkyn placed a high priority on children and their treatment. To hear of a parent treating their children in such a manner would set any sane Dragonkyn on fire with rage.

"The nurse that I talked with at the clinic that the girl goes to said that Aleria is the one that takes her to all of her appointments. She even added that they have tried to contact the parents on numerous occasions and have been hung up on saying that they couldn't be bothered with matters so trivial."

At least Aleria was telling the truth about Sariah. One small thing that made me feel better, but to know that her father and uncle may be high ranking members of the Brotherhood? That made my dragon claw to the surface, raging for revenge against the slight of my people.

"What do you suggest we do now, Klaas?" I sat heavily in the armchair, my head in my hands as my weariness took hold.

He settled a firm hand on my shoulder, squeezing in reassurance. "We need to trust our instincts in this matter. What are they telling you about your mate?"

I hesitated, trying to put into words the feeling surrounding my mate. "I don't believe she wants to harm me, or any dragon for that matter, but she is hiding something. Something that could potentially harm us. It is almost as if they are holding something over her head, forcing her to do something against her will." I ran my fingers through my hair in agitation as the captain looked down at me.

"I agree, and I think it has to do with the sister. I

have already discussed her condition with Drake and he agrees that he would be able to treat her." He paused. "With your permission, I would like to plan an operation to remove the girl from that wretched home."

"What about *Pateros*, don't we need to discuss this with him?"

My father walked through the door giving me a knowing look. "My son, I am already one hundred percent aware of the situation and agree whole-heartedly with Klaas and his assessment, as well as you regarding your little mate." Dimitros stroked his black beard, drifting his eyes between Klaas and I. "While the girl may be hiding something, there is no way she can be that good of an actor to fool us all. Not you, anyway, son." He nodded.

"Thank you, *Pateros*." I inclined my head in appreciation.

"Of course, my son. Now, Klaas, let's rescue the poor girl and get to the bottom of this plot so that we can move on with our lives," he said firmly, authority as king surrounding him.

Klaas smirked, the corners of his mouth lifting in amusement. "Of course, your majesty."

sixteen

ALERIA

THE SUITCASE OPENED AND UNPACKED, I paced the room, scrolling through the messages on my phone. My uncle had sent the information about what it was he wanted me to steal while we were at dinner. The object was a key of some sort, ancient and ornate. I had no idea what kind of door or lock it would go to since it looked to be nine inches long. Etched into the gold, dragons danced along the metal in an intricate pattern of wings and claws.

My mind pictured Xander and what his dragon form may look like. Flashbacks of being burned by a black dragon made me shudder as the memories of the dreams returned to me. I knew I couldn't do this. I had to make it seem like I got the key to them, without betraying Xander. In my heart, I knew it would shatter me completely to do so.

I read through the rest of his messages detailing where the kept the key, hidden in an unassuming box in the library, where no one would actually even think to find it.

How did he know this information? Someone inside the household had to be feeding him information, and I needed to find out who. I needed to fish for some information.

Me: How will I get it to you?

Uncle: You will hide it under a yellow rose bush on the Western lawn outside on Wednesday morning at exactly 9am. My contact will then bring it to me.

Me: If you have someone on the inside already, why did you need me in the first place?

Uncle: No one outside the family is allowed inside that library, hence the need for a whore like you. Remember you have until Wednesday. If that key is not inside the box, Sariah will pay for your failure.

I could imagine his evil laughter at the end of the sentence. Erasing the messages, I sat down on the bed, allowing myself a moment to lament about my situation. Two days was all I had left until the drop off time.

Thinking of who he could possibly have on the inside, I immediately thought of the boy, Daniel, that Xander and I ran into. He looked so familiar because I had seen him at Brotherhood events when he was a child, his parents were very close with my uncle.

I cursed, needing to make sure Sariah was secure before I set my plan into motion.

With a flurry, I began to fire off emails and text messages.

* * *

The door closing softly, followed by footsteps startled me awake. "Xander?" I asked, rubbing my eyes.

"Yes, love." He crawled into bed behind me, wrapping an arm around my waist and drew my back against his chest. "Sorry I'm so late, please go back to sleep." He kissed the top of my hair and my eyes fluttered shut, sleep claiming me once again.

* * *

When I woke, Xander was already gone, causing me to blink in confusion at the empty room. Dinner had seemed to have gone well, and then he disappeared once Ashley showed up. She said my parents gave her a difficult time, but did she suspect anything? I bolted upright, wide awake as terror flooded me. My fingers circled my throat, my pulse racing beneath them. No, he was just an early riser, that had to be it.

"Good morning, sleepy head." His rich voice washed over me as he opened the bathroom door, wrapped in just a towel, water dripping down his golden skin.

Now my pulse was racing for a much different reason. "Good morning," I rasped, my eyes running up and down the length of his body. Heat pooled in my belly. He stalked toward me, his gaze heated as he licked his lips. Setting one knee on the bed, he leaned forward and grabbed the back of my head, kissing me soundly, running his tongue along mine, making me moan deep in my throat.

"That is a pleasant sound in the morning." His

lips trailed down my neck, teeth nipping, tongue tasting me as they blazed a path downward. My fingers tangled in his wet hair as I tried to drag him closer to me.

"Aleria, baby," he breathed against my neck. "I have to go into the office for a bit today. Will you be okay here?" His thumb traced a pattern across the exposed skin just above my hip, causing a shiver to run down my spine.

I pulled back with a frown. "What do you expect me to do all day?"

"You can do whatever you like, there are plenty of movies, TV, books in the library, you can take a stroll of the grounds." More nuzzling of my neck caused my mind to go blank of any thoughts except for him. I wanted him on top of me, his weight holding me down as he drove his cock deep inside me.

"You are trying to make me pliable and more agreeable with sex aren't you?"

"Is it working?" Clever fingers slipped beneath the waistband of my panties, running through my folds before circling my clit.

Arching my back, I made an approving noise in the back of my throat. "Keep doing that and it just might." I felt his lips curl into a smile against my collarbone as he pushed aside the strap of my tank top with his nose.

"Challenge accepted, little mate," he growled, two of his fingers penetrating deep inside of me as his lips clamped around an erect nipple.

He expertly worked my body into a frenzy with his fingers, mouth and tongue. I was at his mercy, a slave to the desires of my body. "Xander, please, I need you inside me," I pleaded on a breathy moan as his fingers continued their assault on my pussy.

"Come for me first," he growled, his voice coupled, with the firm stroke of his thumb over my clit, sent me spiraling over the edge.

He whipped off his towel, pulled my panties down to my ankles and entered me in one swift thrust as the aftershocks ebbed, sending me into another dimension of pleasure. "My *Rashka*," he repeated in my ear, his thrusts growing in their intensity, each stroke had his hard cock rubbing along my clit, sending shockwaves of pleasure throughout my body.

With ease, he gripped my hips and flipped me over onto my stomach, planting a kiss at the small of my back before urging me to my knees. His fingers tangled in my hair, jerking my head back as his cock entered me from behind. I groaned at the feeling of fullness. Lips descended upon my neck, his teeth sinking into my flesh as he resumed his relentless thrusts into my body.

"You are mine, Aleria." His nose brushed along my ear, while his fingers still fisted in my hair aligning me to the exact angle he desired. "Forever and always, *Rashka*." I screamed as the orgasm washed over me, taking me by complete surprise.

His answering groan had my hips bucking wildly as he moved faster and faster into me, his release filling me and prolonging my pleasure, nails digging into the flesh of my hips.

Our bodies drenched in sweat, we both collapsed to the bed, his head resting between my shoulders. "That was—" I groaned into the pillow, my body refusing to obey my commands.

"Amazing, epic, out of this world?" He laughed, feathering kisses down my back as he separated us and drew me into his arms.

My nails lightly ran up and down his abs. "It seems I've gotten you all dirty again after your shower." I bit my lip, giving him a coy look.

"Well then, little mate, I guess you will just have to clean me up."

* * *

Xander's lips lingered on mine as he broke our kiss, "Are you sure you will be okay? I will only be gone a couple of hours." Hands settled on my hips, drawing me closer into his body.

"I'll be fine. I'll probably spend most of the time reading or watching TV. I know you need to get some work done after the whole—" I waved my hands in the air, "—mating fiasco."

His lips quirked as he held back a smile. "I wouldn't call it a fiasco, Aleria. It was a whirlwind, yes, but I do not regret meeting you." His eyes darkened with intensity as he looked down at me, the midnight blue irises drawing me in, pulling me deep under his spell.

"I don't regret meeting you either. Or letting you kiss me," I whispered, toying with the hair on the back of his neck, the soft strands tickling my fingers. "Now go." I skated my hands down to his chest and pushed at the solid wall of muscle.

"Yes, ma'am." He chuckled and gave me a swift kiss before grabbing his keys to head to the garage. I stayed in the kitchen, watching the door for a moment, my plan replaying over and over in my head.

I needed to get the box from the library, switch out the key and place it somewhere safe so that my uncle would never get his hands on it. It was going to be dangerous, I only hoped that the favors I called in would be enough to save Sariah, and that Xander would forgive me for what I was about to do.

XANDER

It bothered me to leave her, even more so after the discussion with Klaas, Ashley and my father last night. But I had to do some damage control today. The press was having a field day, speculating that I had kidnapped the woman and taken her off to my secret lair. Ashley was close to having a mental breakdown after her experience with the evil that was Aleria's family last night; she needed my assistance today.

Thinking over the time that I spent with my mate left me conflicted. Now that I knew what she had been hiding about her family, things started to make more sense. The strange look she gave me after speaking about honesty. When she told me about her virginity so she wouldn't be lying and winced afterward? It had to be because she was lying about so many other things.

My sleek black sports car took the curves of the

country road as I pushed the gas pedal down toward the floor. I was anxious to get to the office, get done what I needed to, and get the hell out of there. I was still in the throes of the mating bond and being without Aleria was making my skin crawl. I only hoped that as a human, she did not feel the same discomfort that I did.

Ashley was waiting for me to arrive, tapping her foot in annoyance as I walked through the door to my office, coffee in hand, wearing this god-awful tie. At least Aleria thought it looked good on me; she said the deep red color complimented my eyes and hair. I reached the cup out to her as a peace offering, which she gratefully accepted, taking a sip with a groan.

"Xander, it has been murder. We have to release a statement today or the press is going to run away with this." She echoed my earlier thoughts.

I pulled out my laptop from its case and booted it up while I took a seat in my chair. "I agree, which is why I already drafted something up last night. You should have it in your email within the next minute or two to proofread and get down to PR," I said, knowing she would be pleased that I had done some fore-thinking before coming in today.

I snarled as I saw that I had over four hundred

unread emails. "How many of these are going to be requests for interviews or photo shoots?" I growled in frustration.

"Most of them," Ashley answered, taking another long drink of her coffee.

"I think I may need one of those too, send one of the interns down the street with the card. Make sure you get orders from the whole floor. I think they are going to deserve it after we clean up this mess." I scrubbed a hand over my jaw as I hunkered down and started going through the disastrous emails.

* * *

"Xander, it's already two. You need to get out of here." Ashley poked her head in, her brow furrowed in concern. "And you haven't had anything to eat. Leave. We have done all that we can for now."

"Damn it," I looked down at my watch, realizing she was right. I ran my hands through my hair, leaning back in the chair to roll my stiff shoulders. How had I let that much time pass? I was planning on getting out of here by noon.

"Here, I had an extra sandwich, please eat it and then get out of here." She set it on my desk and raised her eyebrow at me, leveling a look so fierce, I had no choice but to comply.

"Yes, drill sergeant Ashley." I grabbed the sandwich, tearing it open, and took a bite without even realizing what was in it. Turkey, nice. As I packed my laptop and tablet away, she still stared at me.

"Anything else you would like to add?" I tilted my head.

"Be careful, Xander. I don't want anything to happen to you," she whispered, a tear running silently down her face before she swept it away with a swift swipe of her fingers.

"I will, Ash, don't worry about me." I didn't reach out to touch her, my dragon recoiled at the thought of touching a woman that was not our mate. Instead, I pulled out the packet that I had hidden inside my desk.

"Here, take a look at this over the next few days and let me know your answer. I am probably going to take the rest of the week off, but you know how to reach me." I slid the envelope across the desk. The very one that held her new contract, with the new title, salary, benefits and even the keys to the new car that we had purchased for her.

"What is this?" She hesitated before opening the envelope, gasping as she read the first few lines of the document. "Xander, no, this is way too much," she stammered.

"I won't take your answer now. Read everything over. I will expect a yes when I return next week." I twirled my key ring around my finger, leaving her in stunned silence as she slid into the chair on the opposite side of my desk.

seventeen

ALERIA

I BEGAN in the library when I was sure his car had left the driveway, shutting the heavy doors behind me. I explored the large room, running my fingers along the spines of the books, smiling at the array of genres and collections within the shelves. From the classics, to horror, to westerns, they had it all. The dark oak shelves even had ladders affixed to them to get to the upper racks of books.

A smile on my face lingered as I remembered when Xander first showed me this room. I hadn't seen much because he shoved me against the wall and had his way with me. It was a memorable moment, to be sure, but I did not recall a single detail about the room itself.

Several portraits caught my eye on the opposite

wall. They looked to be of King Dimitros and a woman who had to be Xander and Drake's mother. Her beauty took my breath away. The twins looked very much like their father, but there were subtleties that they took from the mother. The shape of their eyes, the fullness of their lips, even their ears were the same shape. Her white blonde hair was elegantly arranged on the top of her head, her bright blue eyes piercing into the depths of your soul, even from a painting. She was just as Xander had described. Utterly beautiful.

The second portrait was of the four of them together, posed regally, dressed in fine garments that were similar to tuxedos, but slightly different. It had to be shortly before she died because the boys looked to be about the same age as when they arrived on Earth. They were the perfect, happy family.

My heart ached inside of my chest as I squeezed my eyes shut tightly. It would do no good to keep up this line of thinking. I needed to focus. Find the damn key and move on.

Off to the right stood a shelf, but this one did not contain books. It held various mementos: a statue, a hand painted sculpture, and the box that I was looking for, tucked down in the bottom corner. I bent to retrieve it, blowing the dust from the surface. The box was just as well decorated as the key itself, delicate carvings of wings, dragon claws and filigree. The lid creaked as I opened it, the key sitting in a bed of black velvet. I stared at it in wonder.

What could this key go to that made it so very important?

It didn't matter, my uncle would never actually get his hands on it. I closed my eyes with a finality as I took the box, setting out phase one of my plan.

Xander returned home much later than I expected he would. When he said he was only going to be a few hours, I expected him to be back around one as he had left at eight. It was almost three-thirty when he opened the door to his suite and found me curled up on the couch, watching a movie on the large flatscreen TV.

"Sorry that took so long." He sounded tense as he ripped off the tie with a grimace and flung it on the other side of the room, pulling his jacket from his broad shoulders. Leaning down to place a soft kiss on my lips, he smirked.

"What have you been up to today?" he asked curiously before he walked to the closet, changing his clothes.

I craned my neck to get a glimpse of his gorgeous body. When he caught me, a flush rose in my cheeks. His jeans were slung low on his hips, unbuttoned, as he approached me, shirtless. "Are you going to answer my question, little mate?" he said in a low tone, causing me to shiver in anticipation.

I stammered, "I uh—read for a little bit. Helped Hilde make some stuff in the kitchen, then came up here to watch TV." My eyes lingered on his strong chest, the soft, smooth, toned muscles. I wanted to feel them beneath my fingers, his body firm, his skin hot under my touch.

"My eyes are up here, Aleria," he tisked at me, tilting my chin up with his long fingers. He smiled, white teeth gleaming as he unleashed the full power of his devastating grin.

"It's not fair when you do that to me," I groaned, covering my face with my hands.

His laugh intensified as he stepped back. "I'm not doing anything, I have no idea what you are speaking of." He feigned innocence, pulling me to my feet to stand flush against him. His eyes gleamed as he bent down to capture my lips.

"You don't play fair, dragon," I whispered, tangling my fingers through his midnight black strands as I deepened our kiss.

TUESDAY NIGHT

I opened my eyes and adjusted to the darkness, trying to shake off the sleep in my body. Xander had made love to me twice more after we came upstairs after dinner. My muscles were aching, legs shaky as I slowly slid out from underneath him. I had come to realize that he was a heavy sleeper, which worked to my advantage right now.

Wincing as I walked toward the closet, I swiftly grabbed a pair of leggings, tank top and running shoes. I would need to be able to move freely to get the box down to the location for it to be picked up in the morning. Knowing night was my best option, I had hidden the box underneath a giant pile of sheets in the linen pantry. It made for an easy access point.

Giving Xander's sleeping form a lingering look, I swallowed deeply, making my way out of the room. "Please forgive me for my deception," I mouthed, silently praying that he would listen to my explanation when all of this was over.

Tiptoeing down the hall, I recovered the box, and made my way to the back entrance. I had identified the rose bush mentioned by my uncle easily, because it was the only yellow rose plant on the eastern lawn, and it had the perfect little alcove right next to it, perfect for hiding something.

The French doors to the patio opened easily, but I paused briefly, caught in the memory of when I saw Xander standing across the gardens the first night we met. Shaking my head, I descended the stairs and shoved the box into the alcove and started to run back up the steps.

A hand covered my mouth from behind as a large male subdued me, his arms becoming steel bands as they tightened around me. I tried to scream, but the large palm covering my mouth prevented any sound from escaping.

"I am so disappointed in you."

It was Klaas, the captain of the royal guard.

I had been caught.

eighteen

XANDER

LOUD VOICES ROUSED me from my deep sleep, causing me to bolt straight up in the bed as my father bellowed my name. "Alexandros!"

I blinked, rapidly becoming more aware of my surroundings, realizing that Aleria was no longer in bed beside me. Confusion furrowed my brow as I threw off the covers and grabbed for a pair of pants, intent on stopping my father's yelling.

"What, *Pateros*?" I said, opening the door to my bedroom to see Drake, Klaas and him standing in a loose circle around the door, their expressions grim as they would not meet my eyes. "What is going on?" I asked, this time more insistent.

"Where is Aleria?" I demanded, fury pouring out of me as thoughts of my mate consumed me.

"Alexandros, she was caught with the key. We are guessing trying to deliver it to her father or uncle," Father said, his tone softening with pity.

"Where is she?" I bit out.

"In the dungeons," he answered simply. "She has betrayed us son, she must be questioned and then face punishment for her crimes." His voice held a note of bitterness.

My dragon could not be contained any longer, the roar bursting from my chest, causing the furniture to tremble with the ferocity as I ripped open the doors to the balcony and leaped from the second story rise, shifting as I fell. My wings caught me, and I flew off into the night.

My dragon and I tried to process Father's words as we flew across the sky, watching the sun rise over the horizon. There would have to be an explanation for Aleria's treachery. How would she even know of the key or what it would do?

It had been an extreme secret, known only to our family and those closest to us such as Klaas and Hilde. Had someone betrayed them and told the Brotherhood of the secret of the key and the power that it could unleash?

The key was ceremonial, it didn't unlock anything or play any role other than to be ornamental. The real value was the large gemstone at the base of the metal, which when ground and mixed properly became a poisonous substance to all Dragonkyn. In the hands of the Brotherhood, it could be devastating to our people.

After flying for what seemed like hours, I circled back toward the house, realizing that I needed some answers. I landed in the clearing outside the garden, shifting just before my feet hit the soft grass. I strode across the lawn, not caring that I was walking the grounds naked. My thoughts were centered on how I was going to handle this situation, rather than protecting my non-existent modesty.

Drake was leaning against a stone column, waiting for my arrival, holding out a pair of pants for me. I nodded my thanks without saying a word. "I need to go and speak with her immediately, Drake. I need answers." The words were barely more than a growl, my dragon still close to the surface.

"Klaas and *Pateros* have forbidden you from stepping foot on the lower levels until they have questioned her themselves." His hand settled on my bare shoulder. "They know your sympathy for your mate will overrule your common sense and you will more than likely let her go."

I roared. "Not until I have answers!" My fury

overwhelmed me. I needed to know why my mate would betray us like this. And what she knew of the key.

"Calm, brother. We will get answers, but not if you barge in there with a temper. Get your dragon under control." Drake spoke calmly, holding his hands out in front of his body in a show of non-confrontation.

Pacing along the stone walkway, I ran my hands through my hair in agitation. "Drake, I can't calm. My mate is inside our fucking dungeon for stealing the one thing inside this house that could actually kill us."

"I will go and speak with her," he stated finally. "That way you can merge with me and you can gauge her reactions through me."

I raised an eyebrow in question. "Will Father really let you do that?" It was a brilliant plan and would be as if I was almost there. I could speak with Drake telepathically, seeing and hearing Aleria as he questioned her.

He shrugged, as if to say that he didn't care if he would or not. "I will find a way."

"What about Sariah? Were we able to get her out?" I exhaled deeply, still worried about the innocent sickly teenager that Aleria had left behind.

Drake looked stricken at the mention of the poor girl. "Thankfully, she was evacuated shortly before Aleria was caught."

I let my head hang low, "I know Father will do right by her, even with the treachery in her family. She is only sixteen years old and has been ill her entire life," I whispered. My father had more honor than to subject a teen to the sins of her family.

"There is a lot more to it than that, Xander." Drake said, his voice a broken sound.

Eyeing him warily, I cocked my head in confusion. "What is it?"

"Nothing you need to concern yourself with yet, brother." He swallowed, turning his back to me, hesitating with his hand on the doorknob. He looked defeated at the mention of Sariah, but I couldn't figure out why. "I am going to the dungeon now. I suggest you make yourself seen going to your room."

Nodding, I trudged up the stairs to my quarters, to anxiously await my brother's interrogation of my mate.

ALERIA

Klaas had placed cuffs around my wrists before dragging me down the dank stairs to a cellar. He didn't utter a word, his face devoid of all emotion, the scar across his eyebrow making him look even more ruthless. I shuddered thinking of the punishments that they were most likely going to level upon me. I deserved them all. I had lied and tried to steal from them.

The silence was unnerving. I didn't say a word for fear that the large dragon would strike me. Almost tripping as he led me down the dark stairwell, his firm grip on my upper arm was the only thing that kept me from falling. I was sure there would be bruises from his tight grip, but I was grateful not to fall.

A gasp lodged in my throat as we reached a row of cells. This wasn't a cellar or a basement. It was a dungeon.

Withdrawing a set of keys from his back pocket, he unlocked the first cell and pushed me inside. With an overwhelming finality, he closed the door with a loud bang, his silver eyes gleaming in the low light.

"Do you have anything to say for yourself?" his

low gravelly voice whispered, fury rolling off him in waves.

"I want to speak with Xander," I answered firmly, holding my head high even as the tears pooled in my eyes.

"That will not be happening. You will confess your crimes to me or to the King. The Prince will not see you." The Captain crossed his arms over his large chest and narrowed his eyes.

My heart broke at his final words. Xander refused to see me or speak with me. It was as I feared. He would never understand. Lip quivering, I backed away from the bars of the cell to the hard, stone wall. I slid down, the coldness of the bricks seeping into my bones until my bottom hit tiled floor.

"I have nothing to say then." I needed to give my contacts time to get Sariah out. It was my only hope now. When my uncle's inside man didn't find the box where it was supposed to be in the morning, then they would act swiftly in punishing her. The only way that I could hope to save one person I loved was with even that small amount of time.

Klaas nodded grimly. "So be it." He turned on his heel and stomped up the steps, the door leading to the corridor slamming.

Hot tears ran down my face as the room was plunged into darkness.

* * *

Heavy footsteps accompanied by a sliver of light a short time later had me looking up to see who appeared. I held a hand above my eyes as they adjusted to the light, my heart leaping in my throat as I made out a shape that looked like Xander making his way toward my cell. A sob lodged in my throat when his face came into view and I could tell from the cut of his hair that it was Drake.

"I brought you some food." Drake regarded me warily with an arched brow as he placed a paper bag inside the cell and slid it across the floor.

I didn't move from my spot along the wall, staring at the paper bag. My stomach in knots, I was sure I wouldn't be able to eat anyway. "I'm not hungry," I said in a low whisper.

He sighed, walking away briefly before returning with a wooden stool and sat down outside of the prison. He said nothing, just gave me his normal inquisitive stare, crossing his arms over his chest and leaning back.

"Why are you here, Drake? To stare at me? To

torture me?" I growled, tired of the game of chicken we were playing. Being near Drake was making me anxious and miss Xander. I knew it was a foolish notion, he wasn't coming. Would never be coming. He didn't want to see me.

Perfect black eyebrows rose in question, "Aleria, I am here because Xander wants answers and Father will not let him anywhere near you right now." His matter of fact tone had me bristling in surprise.

"This is just a trick to get me to talk," I muttered, burying my head back in my bent knees. Fresh tears sprung to my eyes, but I refused to let them fall.

Drake made an exasperated sound. "No trick, little sister." He held up his hands. "Why did you do this?" he asked, his tone taking on a low note.

"You wouldn't understand."

He just sighed, throwing his arms up. "I am going to guess that they were threatening Sariah."

My head snapped toward him as he said the words. "What do you know of it?" I said through clenched teeth.

The damned dragon just rubbed at his chin as he contemplated what he was going to say. "I am also going to guess that you have no idea what you were actually handing over to your wretched father and uncle. Am I right, Aleria? I usually am, you know."

His white teeth gleamed as he smiled at me, a wicked mirth in his eyes.

"How—" I sputtered, "Did you know about my uncle?"

"We found out two days ago that your family is involved in the Brotherhood. If you had bothered to tell us of your predicament, we would have been able to assist you, but instead you had to do things on your own and muck everything up." He waved his hand and sighed in frustration. "Now Xander is worried out of his mind, furious that his mate betrayed his family and confused with trying to figure out who to be loyal to."

"Damn it, Drake! None of you understand!" I screamed, rising to my feet. "They will kill her and the only thing that I could do was exactly what I did." My face was hot with fury, my hands clenched at my sides. This dragon had no idea of the life that I had been raised in, no idea of the monsters that lived in my house. I was doing this to protect my sister.

"Then make me understand, Aleria." He said, his tone softer this time. "Make Xander understand." His blue eyes blazed into me as he uttered the words.

"My family is pure evil," I spat. "They are

founding members of the so-called Brotherhood for a Pure Society." The name caused a shiver to run down my spine. "I never understood why they hated the Dragonkyn so much. All they," I pinned him with my gaze, "All you ever did was help our society. You were just trying to survive by coming here. What is so wrong with that?" I said in a broken plea.

He nodded urging me to continue. "Sariah has always been sick, and it has always fallen to me to take care of her. My mother is too busy prancing around the house hosting parties or getting too drunk to care and my father and uncle are so involved in the Brotherhood they never notice anything." I turned away, closing my eyes as the memories haunted me.

"When I turned eighteen, I tried to go to college. I was surprised they even let me go." A bitter laugh echoed in the cell. "Within six weeks Sariah had gotten so sick she was in the hospital. Her doctor reached out to me because he hadn't been able to get a hold of my worthless parents to make a decision on treatment. I had to drop out and come home."

The tears of anger fell down my face and I quickly swept them away. "I was the one that made sure the house staff was paid and taken care of, I made sure food was ordered, menus prepared, schedules were done. Yet, they insisted that I didn't do my part to pull my weight around the house."

Drake just sat in silent contemplation as he regarded me, waiting for me to finish. His jaw was set in a firm line as he barely contained his fury at my mention of Sariah's treatment. "My filthy uncle and father demanded that I infiltrate your house," I uttered softly, dropping my gaze to the floor, embarrassment overwhelming me.

"And how were you supposed to do this?" he asked cautiously.

"By seducing one of you. They didn't care which. One, both, it didn't matter as long as I could get what they desired. I was nothing more than a pawn in their ruthless game." My voice began to shake.

A low, menacing growl sounded from his throat, setting me on edge as I lifted my eyes to his. "The moment that I laid my eyes on Xander, I knew was a goner. I didn't know what I was going to do. I had to protect Sariah, but I couldn't betray him. Then my uncle messaged me and said he would harm Sariah if I didn't get the box and the key and place it in the designated area as instructed for their contact to obtain."

I paused, swallowing the lump that formed in

my throat. "Drake, they are going to kill her. I made some calls and did what I could to try and get her out, but I need to make sure she is safe. She is innocent in all of this. Please, whatever happens to me, can you please make sure that she is taken care of?"

"Aleria, if you had just come to us and talked to your mate you would have realized that we were already planning to get you and Sariah both away from your awful family." He exhaled deeply. "Sariah is safe and sound in one of my secure medical facilities as we speak. We extracted her yesterday. She is malnourished and dehydrated, but otherwise fine."

There was a hidden emotion in his words. Desperation. The way that he spoke Sariah's name, with such intensity, his eyes sparkling and his hands clenched into fists. Something else had happened between Drake and Sariah that I couldn't quite put my finger on.

Sobs began pouring out of me and I collapsed to the floor. Relief washed over me at Drake's words. Sariah was safe. Drake would be treating her now, they would care for her as I knew their honor would demand.

Composing myself for a moment, I looked up at him through my wet eyelashes. "The key is hidden inside the black and white vase beneath the chariot painting in the hall outside Xander's rooms."

Drake's eyes widened and his mouth hung open as he blinked at me in shock, "You weren't planning on giving them the key? Then what was in the box, why even place it there?"

"To buy time. I had to play their game, make them think that they were getting the key. It also gave an opportunity for you to try and identify the traitor in your midst."

He closed his eyes as a multitude of expressions crossed over his face. More than once he grimaced as if in pain before his face went blank once again. "Shit. I need to go and talk to my father immediately." He scrubbed his hands over his face before they tangled through his dark hair.

"I had to have the box in the garden by 6am. Keep an eye out for your traitor. Keep my capture quiet if you hope to catch them." I hoped that they would be able to get the person responsible for the betrayal. Even if I would be punished, I would make sure that the true evil ones would be held responsible and pay along with me.

He nodded, brow furrowed as he rose to his feet. "Xander heard you little sister." His eyes, so like my mate's, bore into me, causing my heart rate to accelerate.

"How?" I responded.

He tapped his temple, a soft smirk tilting his lips. "Twin bond, comes in handy in these situations." He tilted his chin toward the paper bag, forgotten in the middle of the cell. "Eat now, we will be back for you as soon as we can." Drake stalked toward the stairs.

He muttered something under his breath, which sounded suspiciously like, "Yes, for maker's sake, I'll tell her," before turning back to me. "My idiot brother says that he is proud of his mate."

Shock washed over me as he shut the door behind him.

nineteen

XANDER

GASPING FOR AIR, I broke the connection I had with Drake and slammed back into my own body. Aleria's words were still ringing in my ears. Of course, my fierce little mate would have come up with a plan to not actually hand over the key. She still didn't even know what it did, yet she stashed it away to keep it hidden from her traitorous uncle.

Fists forming at my sides, I thought of the ways that I was going to enjoy his suffering. Dragonkyn justice would be swift and firm when it came to those that betrayed our people, and the Brotherhood was enemy number one. With the intelligence that Aleria had now provided us, we could start dismantling their evil organization piece by piece.

Quickly mounting the stairs, I retrieved the key

from the vase Aleria said it would be hidden inside and went off in search of my father and Klaas.

Finding them talking in low whispers in father's study, I didn't bother knocking before I threw open the door, slamming the key upon the table before them. Anger and determination driving me, I would prove my mate worthy in their eyes.

"Here is your proof. It wasn't in the damn box the whole time. Aleria hid it, trying to spring a trap that would allow for time to rescue her sister and for us to catch a traitor in our house." My lip curled in a scowl as I looked from my father to Klaas. Their foreheads rose in surprise as they stared at the key.

"And how did you obtain this information, I wonder?" Father said, his mouth tilted in just a hint of a smirk.

"He didn't go near the dungeons, *Pateros*. I did." Drake sauntered in, a smile on his smug face as he pulled out a chair, flipped it around and straddled it.

"Of course, you did," Klaas muttered. "Stupid damn twin connection," he growled, narrowing his gaze at me. I responded with a smirk and a nonchalant shrug of my shoulders. Drake and I had played many pranks on the captain in our youth using the connection and it irked him to no end.

"What is this about a traitor in our midst?"

Father stroked his beard, his eyes blazing with inner fire as smoke swirled out of his nose. Our king had a harsh stance on traitors, which did not come about very often, but they were dealt with quickly and fiercely.

"Someone should be trying to retrieve that box in the early hours of the morning," Drake commented. "Did you remove the box, Klaas?"

The captain snorted as he gave Drake a withering look. "Why on earth would I leave the box outside? That is just irresponsible. Do you think me a fool, young prince?"

"Well, that makes it a bit more difficult to try and capture the traitor," I mused, approaching the wet bar. Pulling out several glasses, I poured each of us a small amount of scotch to help ease the night. It was four in the morning, while we didn't require much sleep, the stress of the evening was grating on us all. I nodded my head at Drake, who took a glass from my hand and passed one to my father and then another to Klaas before accepting one for himself. All three inclined their heads to me in appreciation as they sipped the amber liquid.

"Do you suggest we put the box back?" Klaas said, sarcasm dripping from his tone. The captain did not usually show this much emotion, opting for the stoic, soldiery demeanor, but this evening had brought out his true nature.

"Precisely," Drake smirked.

Klaas growled low in his throat, his eyes turning a deep shade of purple as the pupils elongated, his dragon close to the surface. "You black dragons are impossible," he mumbled, retrieving the box from a shelf in the back of the room and slamming the door behind him.

"Are we done with believing Aleria a traitor?" I asked. My eyes drifted around the room from my father to Drake. I knew Drake believed her innocence, but I didn't know what my father was thinking about her actions. He was a fair and a just man, always listening to all of the sides of the story before making a determination.

Clear blue eyes regarded me with just a hint of pity, his mouth set in a harsh line. "Alexandros, Drakon, I need to hear the entire story that she has shared with you about her family, her upbringing and this cockamamy plan she came up with." He sat down heavily in his chair, resting his chin on a closed fist as Drake shared with him the story that she told him while held in the dungeon.

"Son," he addressed me. "I know that she is your mate and your feelings are biased. What is your dragon telling you?" Leaning forward slightly, he eyed me with rapt attention.

Exhaling deeply, I thought carefully on his question before answering. "When her initial betrayal was exposed, my dragon was angry beyond measure. I knew she was hiding something, I thought that it was because of her family being involved in the Brotherhood." I ran my fingers through my hair as I paced the floor in front of the desk.

"While I flew, I went over her actions. She is scared *Pateros*, and with good reason. Aleria was sent here against her will to seduce and infiltrate our family to steal from us and they threatened the one thing in this world that she cares about the most to do it." My voice rose as anger flooded me. "We shouldn't be angry at her for defending herself and her sister, we should be punishing her so called family for putting her in this position."

My chest heaved and I knew my eyes were glowing with the force of my emotions. "Instead of betraying us," I paused, my throat thick, "Of betraying me, she came up with a brilliant plan to save her sister and catch our traitor, all while not handing over the one thing that could kill us. She doesn't even know what the key is, *Pateros*."

My father nodded in response, the smirk on his face telling me he agreed with my assessment and was going to rule in my favor. "I see your fierce little mate has surprised us all, Alexandros." Pausing, deep in thought, he looked out the window as his eyes clouded with memories. "Your mother would love her fire and the passion with which you defend her."

Jaw clenched, I fought to control myself as the thought that Aleria and my mother would never meet flooded me. His words soothed my soul. He knew her better than anyone; if he told me she would love my mate, then she would. There were many things that I missed about my mother—her rich laughter, warm smile and comforting touch. I know that my mate would have loved her in return and I regretted that they would never get the opportunity.

Looking up, I realized that my father was now standing in front of me as he laid a hand gently on my shoulder. "Son, your mother would be so proud of you both. You have become fine men, honorable and brave. We would expect nothing less from your mate." He pulled me into his arms, holding me close as I squeezed my eyes shut tightly and fisted my hand against his back.

"Thank you, Dad," I said in a broken whisper.

He released me, but held my biceps in a firm grip, his eyes becoming fierce again. "We are going to catch this traitorous bastard and teach him the meaning of Dragonkyn justice." His palms slapped me. I nodded in agreement. "Now, son, go get your mate."

Not thinking twice, I rushed out the door and bolted down the stairs to the dungeon.

I tore the door open and whirled down the steps, cursing the terrible conditions that my mate had been left in even if it was only for a couple of hours. The safe with the keys sat at the front of the room, secured with a biometric lock only accessible with one of the family or Klaas' signature. I quickly pressed my hand to the pad and wrenched the keys from the box.

"Drake, I told you, I have to stay here in order for you to catch the traitor. What are you doing getting the keys?" Her voice was weak and defeated. She didn't even look up, just assumed that it was Drake down here visiting her again.

"I am disappointed in you, little mate." I sauntered over to the cell, placing the key in the lock and sliding the door open with an echoing slide. My eyes were smoldering as I looked her over from head to toe. Her pale form was huddled against the wall, knees drawn up to her chest with her cheek pressed against them, her auburn hair fell like a curtain over her face.

"Xander," Aleria breathed my name, climbing to her feet, leaning heavily on the wall as tears pooled in her eyes. "I—" A shudder ran through her body. "I'm so sorry, please forgive me. When I met you I knew that I could never betray you, I—"

I cut her off, eating up the distance between us in two large strides, taking her face between my hands and slamming my lips over hers. My tongue demanded entrance into her mouth, dominating her, pouring all of my emotions into her as I aligned my body with hers, her breasts pressed against my chest, her hips against mine as her legs lifted and wrapped around my waist. I groaned as I rocked into her softly.

"I love you, my fierce little mate," I breathed against her lips, thumbs stroking the soft skin of her cheeks.

"I love you too, my fiery dragon mate." She smiled back at me, light in her eyes.

epilogue

ALERIA

TWO MONTHS LATER

STRONG ARMS CLENCHED around me as I shifted and tried to wiggle out from underneath his hold. "Xander, I need to get up," I groaned, trying in vain to break his iron hold around my body.

"No, I'm not letting you go," he murmured sleepily, nuzzling his nose into my hair and shifting his hips to press his firm erection into my backside.

"Don't even start that, you know I am spending the day with Sariah going over wedding plans." My protests were feeble as his teeth began to nibble on the delicate skin of my neck.

"Drake can entertain her until then," he growled as he licked a trail along my collarbone.

"What is going on between those two? They argue constantly, I've never seen Drake so frustrated." My brow furrowed in confusion. Sariah and Drake had spent a lot of time together since she had been rescued from my parent's clutches. Drake had found an innovative treatment for her immune disease and Sariah was healthier than she had ever been before. There was something between the two of them, a fire, but Sariah was only sixteen years old so nothing could come of it, right?

Xander chuckled, his chest rumbling against my back as he drew me closer into him. "Don't think on it, little mate."

It had been two months since the incident with the key, Xander and his family forgiving me for the role I played that night. King Dimitros was quite impressed at my plan to catch the traitor.

I had set up the case to project a colored dye the moment it was opened, like those that banks used when catching robbers. Mine was homemade of course using products I had found in the kitchen but was still effective. I was thankful that none of the dragons had opened the case to verify the key was still inside.

The traitor was exactly who I suspected, King Dimitros' personal valet, Daniel. He was only twenty years old, raised within the Brotherhood and he knew nothing but hatred for the Dragonkyn. From a young age, he was groomed and set up to be placed within the household to spy and gather information, feeding it back secretly to the Brotherhood.

When questioned, he had broken easily, spouting off his disdain for the dragons in an almost verbatim speech that the Brotherhood had shoved down the throats of children for years. When Xander told me, I snorted in disgust, having no pity for the hateful boy who betrayed such a loving family.

"I still say we just elope." He slowly pulled the sheet down, exposing my naked body. "It would be so much easier than all of this planning nonsense," he grumbled, fingertips circling around my puckered nipple.

"You know as well as I do that your father, and the world for that matter, would never let us get away with eloping." I arched my spine, pushing my breasts further into his touch and grinding my ass into his firm cock, causing him to growl against my skin.

I found myself flat on my back, my wrists pinned to the mattress beside my head as Xander leaned over me, fire in his sapphire blue eyes. "I know, little mate." His lips parted in a seductive smile, causing me to shiver as his tongue reached out to moisten his lips. Two months later and we still couldn't keep our hands off each other. And from what Dimitros had told me, matings were typically always this intense and remained so as long as the mates lived.

"When I first dreamt of you, my love," Xander stared down at me, emotions close to the surface, "I knew you were my mate. I was terrified because in my dreams I had dropped you while flying."

I gasped at his words. "I had the same dream, Xander," I said softly, causing him to smile in return.

His nose nuzzled along mine, his soft lips placing gentle kisses all over my face. "I know now that dropping you was not literal. Your falling was a rebirth, much like the dreams you had of being consumed by dragon fire. You were reborn stronger and capable of anything. I am honored to be your mate, my Aleria. My *Rashka*."

"I love you, Xander." I whispered, tears pooling in my eyes.

His smile widened, leaning down he pressed his lips to mine. "I love you too, Aleria. Forever."

about the author

Jenn D. Young is a native of Washington, currently living in Arizona. She has always dreamed of writing about the characters that have been floating around in her head. Ever since the age of 14, she has been obsessed with romance novels and reading them as fast as she can get her hands on them. Her first love is Paranormal Romance, but she enjoys stories from all across the genre. You can typically find her listening to music or an audiobook, reading, or hanging out with her dogs Hermes and Loki.

She loves to hear from her readers, so please give her a follow below:

Facebook Reader Group- Jenn's Lost Girls

Amazon

Facebook

Goodreads

Bookbub

Newsletter

Instagram

also by jenn d. young

Reverse Harem Books

Snow Falls Pride Series

A new reverse harem series featuring a different group in a series of interconnected standalones in the small town of Snow Falls, Montana, run by Snow Leopard shifters

Seeking Snow Falls

Storming Snow Falls

Saving Snow Falls

Dark Shifters Universe:

Interconnected with the Snow Falls Pride series, delve deeper into other shifter worlds in a series of interconnected standalones.

Shrouded in the Dark

Emerging from the Dark

Shadows in the Dark (Coming Soon)

Unyielding Fates Series

As balance personified, Atalante holds the weight of the realms upon her shoulders. Together with her four mates, she will eradicate those that seek to disrupt the balance.

Balance Threatened

Balance Altered

Balance Restored

Darkmoor Manor

Angie finds herself the owner of a mysterious manor filled with gargoyles and hidden secrets. Will Hell consume her or will she battle with her monstrous mates to defeat the ultimate evil?

Darkmoor Manor

Curvy Omegaverse

A series of interconnected standalones in a contemporary omegaverse world.

Perfectly Knot

Knot the Only One (Coming Soon!)

Standalones:

Eirlys - Part of the Silver Springs Shared World

Shifting Tides

M/F Books:

The Shadows Ascending Trilogy

Enter a world with demons, vampires and archangels as you've never seen them before. Follow Lorelei and Vincent on their journey of awakening and rebirth as their bond forms and solidifies to save the world as they know it.

Into The Shadows

Out of The Shadows

Embrace The Shadows

Shadows Ascending (The complete trilogy with bonus epilogue)

Dragonkyn Mates Series

The Dragonkyn came to Earth almost a decade ago, seeking refuge from their dying planet. Their numbers decimated, they seek only to survive among humanity. Yet, there are those that seek to destroy them and their fated mates.

Of Love and Dragons

Dragon's Redemption

Standalone Novels

Forbidden Warlock

Love in the Stars - Contemporary Romance

Made in the USA
Columbia, SC
09 June 2023

17762189R00143